"It isn't fair," she said aloud to her reflection in the mirror. It simply wasn't fair that Ryan's parents had broken up, and he'd been moved halfway across the country. Kids didn't have rights when it came to their parents. Except for her, Ryan didn't know a single person his own age. It was up to her to help him make friends. But all her friends thought he was her boyfriend. And if she told the truth, he would probably hate her for it. At the very least, he'd think she was an absolute jerk. She shook her head. What a mess!

Jordan swore she'd make it up to him somehow for all the foolish stories she'd told about him. One way or another, she'd help him every way she could to adjust to his new life. And she'd be certain that he never *ever* discovered the fantastic fibs she'd spread around school about him and their "big" summer romance. She owed Ryan Elliot that much.

Lurlene McDaniel

My Secret Boyfriend

DARBY CREEK PUBLISHING

To my sons, Sean and Erik

Cataloging-in-Publication

McDaniel, Lurlene.
My secret boyfriend / written by Lurlene McDaniel.
ISBN 978-1-58196-008-5

       p. ; cm.
Summary: Jordan Starling enters the eighth grade after an uneventful summer. To compete with one of the popular girls, she makes up a summer romance. The only problem is the "romance" is with Ryan, the son of her mother's best friend. Now Ryan's parents have split up and Ryan and his mom are coming to live with the Starlings.
1. Teenagers—Juvenile fiction. 2. Children of divorced parents—Juvenile fiction. 3. Friendship—Juvenile fiction. 4. Honesty—Juvenile fiction. [1. Teenagers—Fiction. 2. Divorce—Fiction. 3. Friendship—Fiction. 4. Honesty—Fiction.] I. Title.
PZ7.M4784172 My 2004
[Fic] dc22
OCLC: 52907050

Cover Photo by Tanya Dean
Cover design by Keith Van Norman

Published by Darby Creek Publishing
7858 Industrial Parkway
Plain City, OH 43064
www.darbycreekpublishing.com

Text copyright © 1988 by Lurlene McDaniel

Printed in the United States of America

OPM 10 9 8 7

One

"JORDAN! Jordan Starling! Over here!"
At the sound of her name, Jordan searched the swarming halls of students. Everyone was early for the first day of the new school year at Martin Junior High School. The students were all babbling and comparing notes on summer activities. Jordan caught sight of the familiar red curls of her best friend, Laurie Wilcox, and pressed through the crowd toward her. *Being an eighth grader has a certain appeal,* she decided. The shier, more timid seventh graders moved aside for her as she walked through.

When she reached Laurie, she gave her a big hug. "How are you?" Jordan squealed to her best friend. "You look fabulous!"

Over the summer, Laurie had lost some weight. She had a new hairstyle and had shed her glasses in favor of contact lenses.

5

"I'm sorry I didn't call last night," Jordan continued, "but I didn't think we'd *ever* get home. A month in the Rockies is too long to be away from Dallas. We started back in plenty of time, but then the dumb car broke down in the middle of nowhere. It took three days to get it repaired. By the time we got in late yesterday afternoon I had all this unpacking to do, and with today being the first day of school and me having no earthly idea of what to wear or . . ."

Laurie held up her hand to halt Jordan's flood of words. "No problem. I'm just sorry we couldn't get together before now. I've got a zillion things to tell you. And I want to hear all about your vacation. Did you meet anybody new? Did you have fun? What did you do?"

What did she do? How could she tell her best friend that she'd spent four weeks trapped in a rustic cabin with her parents and her ten-year-old brother? She had done nothing but hike, fish, cook, clean, and read.

"Forget me," Jordan hedged. "Tell me all about this guy you wrote about in your letter."

"His name is Wade," Laurie said dreamily. "Wade Matthews. He goes to our school. We've already met and compared class schedules. Our lunch periods overlap so we'll be able to sit together every day."

6

Jordan thought hard for a minute. The only Wade Matthews she could remember was a short, skinny kid who used to sit next to her in sixth grade.

"We literally bumped into each other at the skating rink. I wasn't watching where I was going and *bam*, we collided. At first I started to get mad, but when I stared into his adorable brown eyes . . ." Laurie pressed her brand-new notebook to her chest and sighed.

Jordan had felt that fluttery feeling once in seventh grade over a handsome student teacher assigned to her math class. It was a funny feeling that started in the stomach. Sometimes, it made your head light. It was an awful and wonderful feeling, all at once. But Jordan couldn't imagine feeling that way over Wade Matthews.

". . . and Jennifer added another drooling boy to her list." Laurie's half sentence brought Jordan back to the crowded hallways of Martin.

"Who's the poor creature?"

"Glen Lockwood."

Jordan groaned. Jennifer had been Jordan's rival for years. In almost every area, Jennifer and Jordan competed—honor roll, friends, parts in plays, president of their fifth-grade class, choral soloist in seventh grade—everything!

7

"Guys can be so dumb," Jordan remarked. "You'd think a guy as popular as Glen could find a girl in the ninth grade to care about."

"I guess not."

"I'll have to get the whole story from her," Jordan said, sighing.

"You might as well get it over with as soon as possible. Oops! There's the first bell. We don't want to be late for homeroom." Laurie started backing down the hall as she spoke. "But I really want to hear all about your vacation and any neat guys you met. Okay?"

"Sure," Jordan said, forcing a smile. But there hadn't been any neat guys. What was she going to tell her best friend? That she'd read six books and couldn't remember the plot of any of them? That she'd caught a nine-pound fish, then let it get away because it was too yucky to take off the hook? That the only male she'd seen besides her father and brother was an old man who ran the general store where they bought supplies once a week?

And while she'd gone off into the wilderness to battle boredom and mosquitoes, Laurie had stayed home and met Wade Matthews. And Jennifer had gotten together with Glen Lockwood.

Jordan managed to make it through the

first day of classes and head homeward without running into Laurie again. She didn't want to have to talk to Laurie about a summer romance that never happened.

When she got home, her mother was sitting at the breakfast bar sorting through an enormous stack of unopened mail. "Boy, the junk mail doesn't take a vacation," Mrs. Starling said as Jordan opened the refrigerator and grabbed a can of juice. "How was school?"

"Same old teachers. Same old faces. I didn't really have time to get ready for classes, so I felt lost all day long."

"Stop complaining, Jordan," Mrs. Starling said absently. "You're not the only one who's been inconvenienced because we didn't get home in time from vacation. Your dad's supposed to fly out in two days for a month in the fields."

Jordan's father was a consultant to a large Dallas oil firm and he traveled frequently. He was often gone four to six weeks at a time. But he always brought his family something back from his travels. Jordan had a wonderful collection of dolls that her father had brought her from all over the world.

"Oh, my! Jordan, look at this letter!"

"What is it?" Jordan asked as her mother opened an envelope.

"It's a letter from Beth Elliot. You remember her, don't you?"

Jordan tried to remember the face of her mother's former college roommate. "Sort of."

"We went to college together and even got married within a month of each other. When she got pregnant, I'd thought I'd die if I didn't have a baby, too."

Jordan remembered the familiar story. The two young couples had lived next door to each other in the same apartment complex in Michigan before the Elliots moved to Washington, D.C., and the Starlings moved to Dallas. The Elliots had a baby boy, and then nine months later, Jordan had been born. Jordan and Ryan Elliot had played together in playpens and wading pools and even (heaven forbid!) in the bathtub. Jordan felt a flush of red creep up her cheeks recalling the embarrassing photos in the family album. There were several pictures of her and a pudgy boy with round blue eyes playing naked in frothy bathwater amid rubber ducks and floating plastic boats.

She cleared her throat. "So, what's new with Mrs. Elliot?"

Her mother pulled out the letter and a photo fluttered to the kitchen floor. Jordan stooped to pick it up. A full-length snapshot of "baby"

Ryan made her catch her breath. He wore a T-shirt and shorts, and had muscular arms and thighs. His hair was blond and his eyes, still round and blue, were generously fringed with lush lashes. And his smile was deep and piercing, exposing dimples on either side of his full lips. Ryan Elliot certainly had grown up!

Jordan carefully put the photo on the table, hoping her mother hadn't seen her reaction to the picture. Mrs. Starling's eyes were glued to the pages of the letter. She was frowning slightly. "Uh—anything wrong?" Jordan asked.

"Wrong?" Mrs. Starling said. "Oh, uh—no. Just the usual."

But Jordan knew that something in the letter was bothering her mother. She also knew that her mother wasn't going to tell her about it. Jordan shrugged and scooted away from the table. "Well, I'm going to unpack. If Laurie calls, tell her I'll call her back."

"Yes . . . I'll do that . . ." Her mother's voice trailed off as she returned her attention to the letter. Jordan paused briefly at the table, unable to keep herself from stealing one more look at the smiling boy in the photograph.

She hurried out of the kitchen, wishing she could attract a guy like Ryan Elliot. But she was just the same old Jordan Starling. And she'd never have a boyfriend like Ryan!

Two

"**W**HY don't we meet at the Polar Palace tomorrow after school?" Laurie's voice bubbled over the phone Jordan was holding in her parents' bedroom. "We can compare notes on our summers, and you can meet Wade."

"Sounds fine to me," Jordan lied. Actually, Polar Palace was the last place Jordan wanted to go. The Polar Palace was a popular ice cream shop where all the kids hung out. And she was sure to hear all about everyone's wonderful summers if she went.

After Jordan hung up, she headed to her room and thumbed through her closet, trying to decide what to wear for the second day of classes. The sound of running feet interrupted her. Jamey, her brother, skidded to a halt and stretched his arms across the door frame. "Now don't be scared," Jamey warned, smiling mischievously. "But I can't find Stallone."

"Ugh! That snake gives me the creeps. You'd better find him *fast!*"

"Sh-sh! Do you want to get Mom all upset? He'll turn up. I've already looked all over my room, so I thought I'd check in here next. He could have crawled anyplace, you know."

Nervously Jordan scanned her room's teal blue carpeting. "You find that slimy thing right now, or I'll scream. I'm not going to have that creepy snake under my bed like last time."

"He's not slimy," Jamey said defensively. "He's probably looking for a cool place to curl up. It's hot outside. Besides, Stallone's eaten all his mice and he's probably hungry."

Jordan shuddered. "That's disgusting. Don't you care about the poor little mice?"

"Hey, that's how nature is," Jamey said with a grin. "The strong eat the weak."

"Well, you better find him *now*," Jordan said, not amused.

"Don't get all bent out of shape. Stallone won't bite, you know—even though he might mistake *you* for a rat!"

Jordan shook her fist, and Jamey skittered from the room. She slammed the door and flopped onto her bed. Tomorrow at the Palace she'd have to tell everybody *something* about her dull, boring summer. Laurie had a boyfriend. Jennifer had a boyfriend. But for her, nothing had happened over the summer.

◆ ◆ ◆ ◆

The next afternoon Jordan plastered a smile on her face and bounced into the Polar Palace. The smells of vanilla, chocolate, and strawberry made her stomach growl.

"Hey, Jordan . . . over here!" Laurie was waving at Jordan over the crowded booths. Jordan threaded her way to where Laurie sat with Wade. *He's still skinny*, Jordan thought. She flopped into the bright yellow cushioned booth and grinned pleasantly.

Laurie said, "Do you know Wade?"

"Sixth grade, right?"

Wade blushed furiously and nodded.

"Before I forget," Laurie continued. "I want to sign up for the same activity as you. What's it going to be this year?"

"I heard Mrs. Rose is looking for an editor for the newspaper. I'm going after the job."

"So's Jennifer," Laurie said through a long drag on her soda straw. Then Laurie leaned forward and warned, "Speaking of Jennifer, here she comes."

Jordan braced herself for Jennifer's arrival at their table. The summer had improved

Jennifer. Her wheat-colored hair was a swish of tangled curls. Her green eyes gleamed brightly and her skin was tan. Her outfit reminded Jordan of something out of the newest edition of *Teen Fashion* magazine.

"Well, hello, Jordan," Jennifer said sweetly. "How have you been? Where did you keep yourself all summer?"

Jordan smiled back. "I spent the month of August in the Rockies," she said.

"I wondered where your tan was. I spent two weeks down in Corpus Christi on the beach. The sun must not shine much in the mountains, huh?"

Jordan gritted her teeth. "Mountain air does wonders for the complexion. Sun can turn your skin to leather, you know."

Jennifer's eyes wandered over the threesome. "So, are you waiting for someone special, Jordan?"

"Maybe," she lied.

"Well, did you hear about me and Glen Lockwood?"

"I haven't heard a thing. Is he around?" Jordan looked around at the other booths.

"He's coming here after football practice," Jennifer said quickly. "So tell me about this mysterious boy you're meeting."

Jordan wished she could take back the

careless word. "Well, he's not meeting me here because he doesn't live in Dallas."

Laurie blinked hard at her, but Jordan kept her attention focused on Jennifer. "Oh, you met someone on your vacation. What's he like? What's his name?" Jennifer asked.

Jordan's cheeks burned, and her hands began to tremble. What had she gotten herself into? Then a voice from the far side of the room rescued her. "Hey, Jennifer!" someone shouted. "Glen's here."

Jennifer spun around and caught sight of Glen Lockwood. She waved and then turned her attention back to Jordan. "I've got to run. But I'm dying to hear all the details of your romantic vacation. Maybe tomorrow?"

"Uh—sure. Maybe so," Jordan said as she watched Jennifer flounce off.

"Well, thanks a lot!" Laurie said crossly.

"What's that supposed to mean?" Jordan asked, startled.

"Thanks for not telling me about your new boyfriend. I guess Jennifer has more of a right to know than I do."

Jordan shrugged. "Oh, Laurie, I'm sorry. It's really nothing."

"What do you mean? Did you meet a guy in the mountains or not?"

Jordan looked at Laurie and Wade. Now

16

what was she going to say? She didn't want either of them to think she'd made up such an outrageous story just because Jennifer had ticked her off. "He—he was just some guy in one of the cabins up there . . . and Jennifer sort of irked me. I—I guess I shouldn't have shot off about him. Besides, I'll never see him again, anyway."

By now, her cheeks were flaming. Jordan scooped up her books and stood. "Look, I have to run. Mom's expecting me home to finish unpacking."

"I'll call you tonight," Laurie called as Jordan hurried through the ice-cream parlor and outside into the blazing heat. Once she was outside, she stopped short and breathed deeply.

"What's wrong with me?" she asked aloud. She'd never lied about anything in her life. And now she was knee-deep in a fib about an imaginary boyfriend and a fantasy summer romance. Jordan headed toward the bus stop, chewing her lower lip and mumbling, "What am I going to say now? What?"

Three

"MOM, when am I ever going to change?" Jordan asked as she came through the kitchen door.

"Change? What do you want to change into?" Her mother was standing at the sink shaping hamburger patties. "Dad's grilling outside tonight. Would you please slice some tomatoes onto a platter?"

"Change into a real girl instead of a skinny tomboy."

Mrs. Starling chuckled. "Jordan, you're a very lovely young girl."

Jordan grimaced. "How can you say that? I'm as flat as a board. I could wear postage stamps for a bra and no one would know the difference!"

"You're going to be grown up soon enough. Just enjoy being what you are right now."

"Mom!" Jordan said in an exasperated tone.

Mrs. Starling eyed her critically. "You really are very attractive, honey. Tall, willowy . . . most girls would kill for legs as long as yours."

Jordan turned a full profile toward her mother. "No chest, no bottom, no curves."

Just then, Jamey skidded into the kitchen. He glanced between his mother and sister. "Gee, Jordan," he said with a mischievous grin. "When you stand sideways like that, you look just like my snake!"

"Get out of here!" Jordan shrieked, tossing a wadded dish towel after him as he ran out of the kitchen. "See!" She whirled back to her mother. "Even a ten-year-old can see the difference!"

"Jordan, you know how Jamey likes to tease you. Don't let him get under your skin."

After supper, Jordan retreated to her room to study, but she couldn't concentrate. The lie she'd told about meeting a special guy on her vacation kept nagging at her. Why did she say such a thing? Being jealous of Jennifer was no excuse. Jordan dug out her diary, a beautiful book bound in red leather with ivory-colored pages. She flipped it open and poured out her feelings in black ink. Afterward, she felt better. At least her diary knew the truth.

She locked the book, buried it deep in a

drawer, and tried to study. But all she thought about was how she was going to avoid Jennifer for the remainder of eighth grade.

◆ ◆ ◆ ◆

Jordan made it four days. On Saturday night, Carmen Rodriguez had a back-to-school pool party at her sprawling house. At first Jordan decided not to go since she was certain she'd be the only girl there without a guy. But Laurie begged her, and once she arrived, she realized that most of the kids had come by themselves. Besides, Carmen always had fun parties, and Jordan hated to miss one.

When Jordan arrived, the first thing she did was search for Jennifer, but she wasn't there yet. Good, Jordan thought. *Maybe she won't come at all.* Jordan stood with Laurie on the patio. Wade was in the water with a group of guys. The pool sparkled with underwater lights, and colored lanterns lined the edge of the yard. Music blared over an outdoor speaker system. A table was filled with pizza, chips, colas, and bowls of fruit.

"Scott Lewis is sort of cute," Laurie said to Jordan as she crunched on a small wedge of watermelon.

"Trying to fix me up?"

"Never. Besides, I've waited patiently all week to hear about this boy you met during your vacation. Now's a perfect time."

Jordan's heartbeat sped up. What was she going to say? A commotion from the back porch interrupted her racing thoughts. Jennifer had arrived with Glen. Jordan groaned. *Don't let her come this way* . . . she pleaded silently, but it was too late. Jennifer was headed right toward her.

"Well, hi, Jordan. Hey, Laurie." Jennifer looked cute in a red bathing suit.

"Hi, yourself," Jordan mumbled. She tugged at the leg of her suit, wishing she had a T-shirt or something to put on.

"I thought you'd be here with someone special," Jennifer said.

"Why should she when she has a boyfriend someplace else?" Laurie's words made Jordan cringe.

"Ah, yes. I almost forgot. The one you met in the mountains. What did you say his name was?"

"I didn't."

"And where is he from?" Jennifer's eyes looked mischievous, almost mean.

"I didn't say."

"Well, he does exist, doesn't he?"

"Of course he exists," Jordan heard herself

21

say. "What did you think? That I made him up?" She couldn't believe the words falling from her lips. She wanted to stop them, but it was as if her tongue had a separate brain.

"Don't be silly." Jennifer giggled. "I'm just curious."

Laurie looked at Jennifer with a look that would have frozen a bonfire. "I'm sure Jordan will tell us all about her vacation and the guy she met when she feels like it."

Jordan felt trapped. How could she avoid disappointing her best friend and yet shut up Jennifer at the same time? Then Jordan remembered the photo that had arrived in the letter from Mrs. Elliot. "If you must know, his name is Ryan Elliot and he lives in Washington, D.C. He was staying in a cabin near ours with his family."

"Neat," Laurie offered with an encouraging nod.

Jennifer sniffed. "Washington, huh? Too bad for you that he lives so far away . . ."

Jordan knew Jennifer didn't really believe her. She tried not to care. "It was just a summer thing," she said. "I'll never see him again, so why talk about it?"

"Are we going to stand here and talk all night?" Glen asked.

"Of course not," Jennifer said. She smiled

a fake smile, and looked sweetly at Glen. A sour taste rose in the back of Jordan's mouth.

"That girl drives me crazy!" Laurie said when Jennifer and Glen had headed indoors.

"Just forget her," Jordan said.

"But the way she acted about Ryan! I mean, she acts as if she doesn't believe you. As if you invented him. Boy, she makes me *so* mad!"

Jordan's stomach felt tense. What would Laurie and Wade think of her if they knew the truth? Jordan cleared her throat. "I think I'll go for a swim and cool off." She headed for the pool and dived over the side. The water felt wonderful. She swam several laps, avoiding a throng of other swimmers.

What was she going to do now? She'd told them about Ryan, a boy she hadn't seen since she was a baby. She plunged beneath the water again and kicked her way to the smooth bottom. Then she pushed up and broke the surface. At the same time the photograph of Ryan surfaced in her thoughts. If Jennifer saw the photo, that would shut her up.

Jordan smiled as a plan began to formulate while she swam. Ryan Elliot lived 1,200 miles away. He would never know if she used his photo to get her out of a bind. What harm could it do to show Jennifer his picture?

Four

"MOM! Phone for you! I think it's long distance again," Jamey shouted from the kitchen. Jordan was sitting at the breakfast bar, her books spread out in front of her.

"I'll take it up here in my bedroom," Mrs. Starling called from the top of the stairs.

Jamey waited until his mother's voice came on the line, then clattered the receiver down. Jordan snapped, "Do you have to be so loud about it?"

"Well, excuse me. I forgot there was a genius at work."

"Buzz off."

Jamey stuck out his tongue, then skipped from the room. This was the third long distance call this month and it wasn't her dad calling, either. Jordan wondered who could be calling her mother so often. But she didn't think about it long. She was finally alone in the kitchen. Nervously she licked her lips and eyed the message basket on her mother's desk. One basket held bills, receipts, and memos. The other held letters and other projects her mother had to do.

Jordan knew that somewhere in the bottom of one of the baskets lay Mrs. Elliot's letter. And in the letter was the picture of Ryan. Jordan hadn't had a chance to look for it until just this minute.

She stole across the floor and fingered the stack of papers. Buried in the middle, she found the pink envelope. Gingerly, Jordan fished it out. Her hands shook and her mouth went dry. *I'm not stealing it,* she told herself. After all, Mrs. Elliot had sent the picture for the whole family. And naturally, Jordan had no intention of reading the letter.

She opened the envelope and looked inside. The photo was wedged between several sheets of stationery. Quickly she slipped it out and rested it in her palm. Then she put the envelope back, went to the breakfast bar, and hid the picture in a textbook. Then she scooped up her notebook, papers, and books and carried everything up to her room. She shut the door, then collapsed on her bed.

She'd done it! She'd gotten the photograph. Carefully Jordan flipped through the book until she found Ryan's picture. She held it beneath her desk lamp and looked at it carefully. Ryan Elliot was even more good-looking than Glen Lockwood, she thought.

She got her purse and carefully slid the picture into a clear plastic holder in her wallet. Then she smiled to herself. Phase one of her plan had gone off without a hitch. Now it was time to begin phase two.

◆ ◆ ◆ ◆

"Jordan, congratulations on being chosen for editor." Carmen's friendly words caused Jordan to glance up from her position at the card catalog in the school library.

"Thanks. You'll be working with Laurie and me, won't you?"

"You bet. And don't forget . . . so will Jennifer," Carmen said with a smug giggle. Jennifer had been surprised that Jordan had been chosen over her as editor of the school paper. Mrs. Rose had made the announcement the day before.

"How could I forget?" Jordan said. "Jennifer keeps giving me dirty looks." Jordan's smile was broad. "But I can take it."

Actually Jordan was more interested in Jennifer at that moment than in Carmen's warm wishes. Jennifer was seated on the far side of the library. From her position at the card catalog, Jordan could see her every move. Pretending she was interested in the index cards she was holding, Jordan nonchalantly glanced toward the table where her own books and papers were heaped. To the casual observer, it was just a pile of study materials. But to Jordan, it was a carefully laid trap.

On top of the pile lay her wallet, flipped open to the photograph of Ryan. All someone had to do was walk past the table and look down. A frown knitted Jordan's brow. Why didn't Jennifer move? Suddenly Jennifer glanced up, and Jordan quickly buried her nose in the cards. Then Jordan looked back and saw Jennifer stand, stretch, and amble through the maze of study tables.

When she reached Jordan's books, Jennifer paused and glanced in both directions before looking down. Jordan had her! Like a fish in a net! Jordan walked up from behind and said, "Can I help you, Jennifer?"

Jennifer whirled around. "I—I—uh . . . I saw your wallet laying here and I was afraid someone might steal it."

With exaggerated slowness, Jordan picked up the billfold. "You're right. How careless of me." Jordan paused, held up the photo section, and asked, "Did I ever show you this picture of Ryan?"

"No," Jennifer said stiffly.

"Maybe I forgot. Anyway, here he is." She dangled the picture under Jennifer's nose. "He's cute, huh? Oh, well, what does it matter? He's so far away, we'll never see each other again. But it's fun to dream, isn't it?"

Jennifer's smiled looked forced. "Maybe he'll write," Jennifer said.

"Maybe," Jordan said as she shut her wallet and put it away. "But after all, it was just one of those crazy summer romances. Perhaps you'll have one next year and you'll understand what I mean." Jennifer's cheeks turned red, but she said nothing. "I've got to run," Jordan added, picking up her stuff. "See you at the newspaper staff meeting tomorrow."

"Sure. See you."

Jordan left Jennifer standing, and scurried out the door. She'd done it! She'd actually proven that Ryan existed. She ignored all her white lies that had gone into creating her "romance" with him. Now she could return the photo to her mother's letter. Now everybody could get on with the school year and forget about Jordan Starling's big summer romance.

28

She breathed a sigh of relief. It was finally over.

Still, she did have the photo in her wallet. And Laurie and Carmen hadn't seen it. Maybe she'd let them sneak a peek before she returned it. After all, they were her friends.

Jordan hurried down the hall to look for them. She'd show them the picture, then let the whole episode die down. And she'd never, *ever* tell another fib again as long as she lived!

◆ ◆ ◆ ◆

As editor of the school paper, Jordan found herself busier than ever. *The Martin Tattler* was published once a month. Stories had to be gathered and written and then rewritten and edited. After final approval by Mrs. Rose, the newspaper had to be pasted up and approved, then sent to be copied. Being editor was a big job, but Jordan enjoyed it, especially the pasteup part. As editor, she directed the staff, telling them what jobs they had to do. She tried to be fair and not act too bossy, but it was fun knowing she was in charge.

Jordan gathered her staff to put the final touches on the September edition in Mrs. Rose's room. She reread the interview she'd done with Glen Lockwood, chuckling to herself as she remembered the day she'd done the interview. She'd taken notes while Jennifer had seethed silently in the background. Actually, the interview had proven to be a real eye-opener to her. For all his good looks, Glen wasn't very fascinating. He was boring! All he could talk about was football. She'd had a hard time writing an interesting story about him.

As Halloween approached, Jordan thought her mother's mind seemed to be elsewhere. And her mom spent many hours on the phone. Mr. Starling left for the Orient for three weeks and promised to bring lots of gifts back for Christmas. But her father's parting words to her mother at the airport when they drove him to catch his flight left Jordan even more confused. He had said, "Do what you think is best about that other situation, honey. I know how important she is to you." Jordan thought about what he said, then shrugged it off. Grown-ups sometimes said strange things that didn't make sense.

The Sunday before Halloween, the skies turned gray and the air held a frosty chill. Jordan snuggled on the couch in the family room and watched the Cowboys play football on TV. Jamey lay on the floor, a bowl of popcorn within reach.

The newspaper was ready to be copied—ahead of schedule—Jordan thought happily to herself. Her research was finished on her English paper and it wasn't due until the following Friday. And the Cowboys were killing their opponents.

Jordan was reaching for a handful of popcorn when her mother walked briskly into the room and snapped off the TV set.

Jamey bolted upright. "Hey! We were watching."

"You can turn it back on in a minute," Mrs. Starling said. "But first I want to talk to both of you."

Impatiently Jordan searched her memory for any rules she might have broken. She drew a blank. She'd even picked up the heap of dirty clothes from her closet floor that very morning. It must be something Jamey had done.

"I'm sure you're aware of how much time I've been spending on the phone lately," her mother began.

Jamey nodded. "You're on it more than Jordan. And she's *always* gabbing."

Jordan made a face at him. "Okay, so you've been talking a lot. Who to?"

"I've been talking to Beth Elliot." At the mention of the name, Jordan sat up straighter and swallowed. Mrs. Starling continued. "Poor Beth's going through some very bad times. I'm sorry to say that her marriage has broken up."

Jordan didn't know what to say. Her mother sighed. "Beth isn't doing very well, and I think she needs to get out of Washington." An uneasy tingling started in Jordan's stomach. "So I've asked her and Ryan to come to Dallas. And to stay here with us for as long as it takes for her to get herself together."

Five

JORDAN was so stunned she could hardly breathe. Ryan Elliot was coming to live in her house! Ryan—her secret boyfriend.

Mrs. Starling's eyes looked misty. "Beth is my best friend, and she's going through an awful time. Ryan, too. I think we can help them get back on their feet. What do you think?"

Jamey shrugged. "Sounds all right to me."

Jordan said, "No!"

Her mother gasped. "What did you say?"

"N—no problem . . .," Jordan quickly added.

"I knew I could count on both of you. I've got most of the details worked out. We'll put Beth in the guest room and Jamey, you'll have to share your room with Ryan. Is that all right?"

"Neat!" Jamey exclaimed. "It'll be like having a big brother."

Jordan couldn't trust her voice, so she said nothing. Then Mrs. Starling added, "Beth was once an excellent legal secretary. I'm sure she can find a good job in Dallas. And a nice apartment, too. But until then, she and Ryan will live here with us." She directed her next remarks to Jordan. "It won't be without adjustments. The three of you will have to share the upstairs bathroom—"

"No more undies on the shower-curtain rod," Jamey interrupted.

Jordan felt color stain her cheeks. Her undergarments were the least of her worries. "When are they coming?" she managed to croak.

"Right after Thanksgiving," Mrs. Starling said. "That way Ryan will have a few days to settle in before school starts again. He's a very good student and a basketball player, too."

"Basketball!" Jamey yelped. "Oh, boy!"

"He—he'll be going to Martin?" Jordan's voice sounded squeaky.

"Naturally. He's in eighth grade, just like you. I'm sure you can introduce him around to all your friends and make him feel right at home." By now, Mrs. Starling was beaming. All Jordan felt was a sick feeling in her stomach. This couldn't be happening! What was she going to tell everybody at school?

"Now we've got lots to do before the holidays, so I expect both of you to pitch in and help."

Jamey nodded eagerly. Jordan just stared. "In less than four weeks, Beth and Ryan will be living with us. I can't wait!" Mrs. Starling added.

That night, Jordan couldn't sleep. She tossed and turned and pounded her pillow into a lump. How had this happened to her? Would she ever be able to put this stupid lie behind her? Why had she allowed Jennifer to shame her into making up a fib about a boy she didn't even know in the first place? "Summer romance!" She spat out the words and muffled them into her pillow.

Finally, she got up, flipped on her lamp and dug out her diary. She poured out her anger and frustration as fast as she could write. Writing in a diary didn't solve her problem, but it did make her feel better. Jordan sighed, put the book away, and turned out the light. An hour later, she finally fell asleep.

◆ ◆ ◆ ◆

The next day, Jordan couldn't concentrate on the newspaper. All around her, the Martin newspaper staff scurried and scrambled, putting together the November *Tattler*. Long worktables were littered with scraps of paper, sports photos, story ideas, and a computer diskettes.

"Well . . . is my story about the new teachers this year on the front page or not?" Laurie's question startled Jordan.

"What? Oh—uh—sure. Yes, it is."

"Jordan, what's wrong with you? You've been in outer space all day!" Laurie sounded irritated.

Jordan closed her notebook. "Sorry. I've just got a lot on my mind."

Laurie's eyes narrowed perceptively. "Are you all right? Are you in love?"

"Who's in love?" Jennifer piped in from across the table.

"No one," Jordan snapped.

"Laurie's right, Jordan," Carmen interjected. "Something's bugging you. Why don't you tell us?"

"Maybe later," Jordan mumbled. "We have to get to work on the paper right now." In minutes, she was busy with her work. An hour later, Jordan had the outline for the November issue ready.

"Not bad," Jordan said, standing swiftly and depositing the outline on Mrs. Rose's desk. Now Jordan focused on getting out the door with no more questions from her friends. But she wasn't that lucky.

"Now come over here and sit down and tell us what's going on with you." Laurie patted a desk chair invitingly. Carmen and Jennifer dragged their chairs over to form a cozy little circle. Jordan felt like lead weights were tied to her feet, but she managed to drag herself over. She felt like the mice Jamey fed to his snake—trapped and waiting to be eaten.

"It—it's about Ryan . . ."

"That dreamy guy you met last summer?" Laurie asked.

"What about him?" Jennifer asked.

"Well, I didn't exactly meet him in the mountains." Her friends were silent. "I mean, I knew him from a long time ago." They just stared blankly. "His mother is a long-time friend of my mother's and now his parents are getting a divorce—"

"The guy from your vacation is really an old friend?" Jennifer interrupted. "You've lost me."

"Sort of. I met him when I was much younger."

"Oh, I get it," Laurie said, snapping her fingers. "Your family and his are old friends and so you spend your vacations together in the mountains."

"Not quite . . ." Jordan squirmed.

Carmen said, "I saw his picture and he's absolutely gorgeous, so I don't care where you met him. Most of the sons of my mother's friends look like cavemen." She crossed her eyes and everybody laughed.

"What exactly do you want to tell us about him?" Jennifer asked, forcing attention back onto Jordan. "If he's really a former friend, so what? What's the big news about him and you right now?"

She's enjoying every minute of this, Jordan thought sourly. But she took a deep breath and plunged ahead. "His parents are splitting up. So my mother's asked Ryan and his mother to move in with us."

Six

FOR a minute no one spoke. Then everyone spoke at once.

"Too much!"

"Wow!"

"That's really neat!"

Confused, Jordan glanced from face to face.
"What do you mean?" she asked.

"How can you sit there looking innocent
when you know that your boyfriend is moving
here?" Laurie burbled.

"Yes, but . . ."

"But what a neat thing to happen!"

"It is?"

"Don't you play innocent with us, Jordan
Starling," Carmen scolded. "You mean to tell
us that Ryan, the guy of your dreams, is
actually moving here?"

"Well, yes, but . . ."

For once, Jennifer had nothing to say. She

only sat, wide-eyed, listening.

Carmen forged ahead. "Imagine living under the same roof with your very own boyfriend." She faked an exaggerated swoon. "How *romantic*."

Jordan's brain began to whirl. Her friends weren't laughing at her! Why they'd hardly heard the part about her summer vacation where she tried to confess the truth about *not* meeting him in the mountains. All they could talk about was that he was moving here. She couldn't believe how lucky she was! Of course, they still thought that Ryan was her boyfriend, but she'd clear that up some other time.

"Calm down," she warned her friends. "It's been a long time since we've seen each other and I have no way of knowing how he feels about me."

Laurie dismissed Jordan's comment with a wave of her hand. "If you were crazy about each other this summer, then the feelings will return."

"I can't be sure." Why didn't her friends back off? She didn't want to make up any more wild stories she'd regret later.

"You'll know for sure in a few weeks," Jennifer said, giving Jordan a skeptical look. "Who knows how you'll feel about each other when he arrives? Too bad you haven't been writing all this time. That way you'd have some idea."

Jordan's blood ran cold. Trust Jennifer to think of the one thing that could expose her made-up stories. "You're right. We'll just have to wait and see." Jordan scooped up her books, suffered through another round of good wishes from her friends, and then beat a hasty retreat to the bus stop.

◆ ◆ ◆ ◆

Jordan couldn't remember ever dreading a holiday more than that particular Thanksgiving. Ryan and his mother were arriving the next day and Jordan still hadn't told her friends the truth. Even having her father home to carve the turkey didn't make up for how rotten she felt. "More mashed potatoes?" her dad asked from his chair at the head of the table.

"No, thanks," she mumbled.

"Are you all right?" her mother asked. "You've hardly eaten anything!"

Jordan quickly smiled at Mrs. Starling. "I'm just fine. Maybe I nibbled too much when I was helping you cook."

"I hope that's all it is. Goodness, we don't need you getting sick with Ryan and Beth coming tomorrow." Jordan's mom frowned.

"Right. I sure don't want to get sick."

Jamey piped up from across the table with, "Gee, just looking at her makes me sick."

"Not funny, young man," Mr. Starling told him with a note of warning in his voice. He directed his next words at his wife. "I'm sorry I won't be able to hang around the airport until their plane lands, but mine leaves for Germany earlier in the day. I tried to postpone the trip, but I couldn't."

"How long will you be gone this time, Dad?" Jordan asked half-heartedly. She'd been too preoccupied with her own troubles to think much about her father's upcoming business trip.

"Until mid-December. I'll be home for Christmas."

"You'll have plenty of time with Beth and Ryan then," his wife assured him. "I don't care if they stay with us forever."

"Me either," Jamey interjected. "Do you think Ryan will like my snake?"

Jordan rolled her eyes. "All boys like snakes," she said meanly. "After all, that's what you're made of—snakes and snails and puppy-dog tails."

"Well, it sure beats sugar and spice," he countered.

"Now you two stop bickering," Mrs. Starling directed. "I want us to be thankful for each other."

"I'm thankful," Jamey insisted. "I'm thankful there's another boy moving into this house tomorrow."

Jordan stuck out her tongue. It was bad enough that Ryan was showing up on her doorstep, but what if he was as much of a pest as Jamey? What if she hated him?

Her kid brother was a nuisance, but she didn't realize how much of one until later that day when she entered her bedroom, lost in her thoughts. She heard snickering coming from under her covers. She flung back the comforter and found Jamey buried in the sheets with a flashlight and her diary. "You sneak!" Jordan exploded.

Jamey tossed the book aside and scrambled beneath the bed.

Jordan dropped to all fours and attempted to grab hold of him. "How dare you read my personal diary! You know the rules." The family rules had always been very firm. Private property was off-limits. No one could borrow without permission or snoop in another's things.

Jamey scooted away from her. "It was an accident," he whined.

"An accident! You were deliberately reading my diary."

"Well, you shouldn't have left it open on your bed . . ."

"That's no excuse. Come out here right now."

"Only if you promise not to hit me."

"Hit you? You'll be lucky if I don't *kill* you!"

Jamey again scooted away from her grasp. "Let me out from under the bed and we'll talk about it," he bargained.

Jordan knew it was impossible to grab him, so she stepped back. Jamey climbed out, but kept the bed between him and his sister. "We're going downstairs right this minute and tell Mom what you've done. You know how she feels about sneaks."

Jamey's brown eyes had grown wide with fright. "If you tell on me, then I'll tell on you."

Jordan paused, a prickling sensation shooting up her spine. "What do you mean?"

"You're the sneak," Jamey accused. "I read what you said about Ryan to all your friends."

Jordan gasped.

"I just read a few pages," he added hastily. "I didn't read the whole book. If you don't tell on me, I won't tell on you."

Jordan was trapped and she knew it. "You're a real brat, Jamey Starling. But I may let you off this time," she said grimly.

A smile full of mischief lit up his face. "Then it's settled. You don't tell and I won't tell."

She hated to give in to him, but she knew she had no choice. "Just get out of my room," she ordered.

Jamey sauntered toward the door and then paused. "Of course, I figure you've got more to lose than I do."

"What do you mean by that?"

"I mean it may cost you something for me to keep my mouth shut."

Jordan studied him through narrowed eyes. "Don't play games, Jamey."

"I've got kitchen clean-up this week and I want you to take it for me," Jamey said.

"No way!" she exploded. "That's blackmail!"

"It's negotiation," he corrected. "I see them do it on TV all the time. You trade in an old car and bargain for the price of a new one. Then after you negotiate, you compromise," he added. "How about kitchen duty for the next three days?"

She weighed the alternatives. She didn't want her parents to find out about all her fibs and fantasies about Ryan. She didn't want to give in to Jamey either. But it was the lesser of the two evils. "Three days," she told him through gritted teeth. "Just three days."

A bright smile lit up his face. "My lips are sealed."

Jamey scampered from the room. With

shaky hands, Jordan retrieved her diary, locked it, and buried it in the deepest drawer of her bureau. Maybe it would be best if she never wrote in it again. But then who would she tell her thoughts to? She couldn't tell her mom. Or even Laurie. There was no one. And confessing to the diary had given her some sort of outlet. Oh, why had she ever opened her mouth in the first place?

Seven

THE Dallas airport teemed with holiday travelers. There were people everywhere, loaded down with souvenirs and luggage. Jordan sat rigidly in a padded chair, her heart thumping hard in her chest. The plane from Washington had arrived, and it was only a matter of minutes before the Elliots walked into the terminal.

Mrs. Starling was too excited to sit still. Jamey kept busy at a nearby video game. Back at home, their house had been thoroughly cleaned. The guest room had been aired, and a bouquet of flowers had been placed on the dresser. Bunk beds had been assembled in Jamey's room. His closets had been half emptied, and a new dresser had been added. Everything was ready—except Jordan. She dreaded Ryan's arrival more than a visit to the dentist.

"There they are!" Mrs. Starling shouted. "Beth! Here we are, Beth!"

Mrs. Elliot was blond and stylishly dressed in a pale blue wool suit. Behind her came Ryan. He was tall and serious and carried a duffle bag over his shoulder and a small suitcase in his hand. He was even better-looking in person than in his picture. "Hi," Jordan said.

"Hello," he answered stiffly.

The two mothers embraced and reintroduced their children to each other. Jordan thought Beth Elliot was pretty, but she had tired lines around her eyes that made her look older than she was.

"We'll get your luggage," Mrs. Starling directed. "Oh, Beth, it's so good to see you."

"It's good to be here," Mrs. Elliot said quietly.

They headed down the escalator to the baggage-claim area. Jordan followed Ryan through the crush of people, watching his back weave through the crowds. Jamey had to run every couple of steps to keep up with him.

In the car, heading for home, the three of them sat in the backseat, while the mothers chattered up front. Jordan gave Ryan a sidelong glance. He'd dropped his head back against the seat and closed his eyes. He looked tired and alone.

Jordan tried to imagine how he must feel. His parents were divorced. He'd had to pack and move hundreds of miles away from his friends and school. And now he had to live with strangers. The thought brought a lump to her throat.

"I've got a snake." Jamey's timid voice broke the strained silence in the backseat. "Did you ever have one?"

Ryan opened one eye and peered down at Jamey's face. "No. I've never had a snake."

"Jordan's afraid of Stallone. But he's really a very nice snake. I'll let you hold him whenever you want. When we get to the house, I'll show you."

"I don't think I want to mess with your snake," Ryan said, his voice low.

"Oh." Jordan could hear the disappointment in Jamey's voice.

Ryan looked at Jamey briefly, then added, "Maybe some other time."

"All right!" Jamey beamed, and a tiny smile turned up the sides of Ryan's mouth.

At the house, they unloaded the car and Jamey led the Elliots on a tour of their new home. In Jamey's room, he proudly showed Ryan his new bed. "Can I have the top bunk?" Jamey asked shyly. "I didn't want to take it in case you wanted to sleep on top."

"Sure, sport," Ryan said, turning his face away quickly.

What a weird turn of events to have brought him back into her life. Too bad it had to be this way, instead of the way she'd told all her friends. But it *was* this way. Like it or not, Ryan Elliot was living in her house.

◆ ◆ ◆ ◆

Jordan took a phone call from Laurie in her mother's bedroom late that same afternoon.

"So how's it going?" Laurie burbled.

"How's what going?" Jordan asked.

"You know—the reunion between you and Ryan. Is the magic still there from this summer?"

"Good grief, Laurie," Jordan snapped. "He's only just arrived. We've barely had time to talk."

"Well, don't bite my head off," Laurie pouted. "I was just wondering."

Jordan sighed. Was she ever going to be able to get out of the lies she'd told? "Look, I didn't mean to sound so snippy, but Ryan and I aren't . . . I mean, we're just different from you and Wade."

"I can tell that. Look, I'll wait until school starts to meet him. That way you two can have plenty of time to get to know each other again. Maybe by next Monday that old magic will be back."

A sinking sensation settled in Jordan's stomach. *School.* "Sure. Maybe I'll introduce you and Ryan at school. And thanks for understanding." She hung up, relieved. She wouldn't have to think about her problem with Ryan and her friends for another week. In the meantime, she'd do whatever she could to get to know him, because Monday would be here before she knew it.

◆ ◆ ◆ ◆

The chatter around the dinner table that night was lively as the two mothers rehashed old memories. "Remember how they used to sit in their high chairs together and throw food at each other?" Mrs. Starling laughed as she passed around a platter of fried chicken.

"And remember the time that Jordan turned her bowl of spaghetti on top of Ryan's head?" Mrs. Elliot added.

"Or how about the time he grabbed her ice-cream cone and smeared it all over her face?"

Jordan groaned, and Ryan just shrugged.

"And remember how they held World War III in the bathtub every night over Ryan's rubber duck?" Mrs. Ryan asked, laughing.

"How can I forget?" Mrs. Starling chuckled. "I even went out and bought Jordan her own toy duck, but only Ryan's would do."

At the mention of their baths together, Jordan felt her face grow hot with embarrassment. Ryan rolled his eyes and glanced away.

"And do you remember Ryan's first haircut?" Mrs. Elliot continued. "The barber cut off all his blond curls, and Jordan started wailing and picking up the hunks of hair, saying, 'Put back!'"

Mrs. Starling nodded. "I don't know who was crying harder, Beth. You or Jordan."

"Well, it was his very first haircut," Mrs. Elliot said defensively.

"Look what I found," Jamey interrupted, carrying an old photo album toward the table.

To her horror, Jordan saw that it was opened to scenes of herself and Ryan playing in a wading pool, stark naked. Jordan almost screamed. But Ryan gently took the album and shut it without bothering to glance down. He said, "Later, sport. I think your sister and I are bored with these stories. Didn't you tell me you had a snake?"

"You bet! Follow me."

Jordan watched the two of them leave the kitchen. She was grateful to Ryan for changing the subject. He must have been just as embarrassed as she was!

Jordan went to her room and thought about the information she'd learned about Ryan. Naturally, she didn't remember any of the incidents their mothers had shared, but it sounded as if they'd spent a great deal of time together as babies. Fighting over a rubber duck! It did sound pretty funny.

"It isn't fair," she said aloud to her reflection in the mirror. It simply wasn't fair that Ryan's parents had broken up, and he'd been moved halfway across the country. Kids didn't have rights when it came to their parents. Except for her, Ryan didn't know a single person his own age. It was up to her to help him make friends. But all her friends thought he was her boyfriend. And if she told the truth, he would probably hate her for it. At the very least, he'd think she was an absolute jerk. She shook her head. What a mess!

Jordan swore she'd make it up to him somehow for all the foolish stories she'd told about him. One way or another, she'd help him every way she could to adjust to his new life. And she'd be certain that he never *ever* discovered the fantastic fibs she'd spread around school about him and their "big" summer romance. She owed Ryan Elliot that much.

Eight

"**D**O you jog?"

Ryan's question startled Jordan. She lay curled up on the sofa, reading the Saturday morning funnies, still wrapped in a terry-cloth bathrobe and oversized, fuzzy pink slippers. Ryan was dressed in a gray sweat-suit. A white headband held a thatch of blond hair off his forehead. "Are you kidding?" she joked. "My idea of exercise is getting the morning paper from the end of the walk. Besides, it's forty degrees out there."

"Oh. I was just wondering . . ."

Then she noticed his downcast expression. Suddenly, it hit her that he probably jogged often and that he didn't know a thing about her neighborhood. "Uh—wait a minute. Maybe I could be persuaded to take a few laps with you. I could show you the way to the park."

Ryan smiled slightly, showing his dimples. "Thanks. I'd like that," he said.

She quickly changed into a baggy pink sweatshirt, jeans, heavy socks, and a ski cap.

Outside, an overcast sky and chilly breeze made her shiver. Why had she ever agreed to this insanity? Ryan said, "You look sort of athletic, that's why I asked if you jog." Little puffs of vapor came out with his words.

Jordan laughed out loud. "Tell that to my gym teacher. She says I run like a klutz. I even trip over my own shadow."

"Then I won't push too hard. We'll take it nice and easy."

"The park's two blocks up and two blocks to the right."

"Let's go." He started off running and she bolted after him, the wind stinging her eyes and numbing her nose. After less than a block, Jordan could scarcely breathe. Her lungs felt as if they were on fire, and her legs were rubbery. Ryan turned and jogged backward, grinning at her. "Feels great, huh?"

"Yeah, if you . . . like ice blocks . . . for hands and . . . feet," Jordan said, out of breath.

By the time the park came into view, Jordan was sure she would drop dead. At the edge of the park, Ryan paused and Jordan leaned over, resting her palms on her knees, gulping in mouthfuls of air. "Is this your park?" Ryan sounded disappointed.

She scanned the area. A softball diamond stood at one end, and there was a playground at the other. "This is it. What's wrong?"

"It's just kind of"—he searched for a word—"empty. I mean, back in Virginia there are so many trees."

Jordan knew what he meant. The park *did* look lonesome and bare. "I guess if you're used to lots of trees, it is sort of . . . barren."

He started running again, heading toward the concrete playground. Jordan followed him. When he reached one of the benches, he stopped to rest and motioned for Jordan to sit down. "Do you like living here?" he asked.

She shrugged. "I don't ever remember living anywhere else. Dallas is home."

"You mean you don't remember dumping spaghetti on my head?" His eyes twinkled.

"And baby Ryan, why would you smear ice cream all over my face?" She picked up his teasing tone. "A nice kid like me. And how dare you not share your rubber duck!"

"I don't share my rubber duck with anybody." He chuckled for the first time since he had arrived. "How long do you think our mothers are going to keep dragging out those old memories?"

Jordan wrinkled her nose. "Probably forever. My mother loves to talk about the times we were babies together and living next door to your mother. She says everybody was poor but happy."

"Well, one good thing. Mom's laughed more in the past two days than she did in the last six months in Virginia." His eyes hazed over, and lines creased his brow. "It's good to see her laugh and have a good time again."

"Were things really bad?" She asked the question hesitantly, because she didn't want it to sound as if she were prying.

"When Dad and Mom weren't yelling at each other, Mom was crying. She cried a lot. Dad told me he'd never leave, but he did. People make you believe they care about you, but they lie."

Jordan squirmed, thinking of the lies she'd told her friends about her and Ryan. "Maybe they don't mean to. Maybe it just happens."

Ryan scoffed. "A lie's a lie. It doesn't matter what you *mean*. It only matters what you *do*."

A silence fell between them. Jordan cleared her throat, anxious to change the subject. "Want to head back? We don't want to miss breakfast, do we?"

He smiled, brightening the dark mood between them. "I never want to miss breakfast."

He started to jog. "Besides, who would I throw my eggs at?"

She fell into step next to him. "Yeah . . . who?"

After their jogging session, Ryan kept to himself the rest of the day. Jordan understood. Everyone in her family was a stranger to him, including her. But she wanted to get to know him better. She wanted him to like her home and his new life. And she wanted to help him fit in.

But there was school on Monday. How would she act when all her friends asked her questions about him? What would she do if Ryan found out about the lies she'd told? Jordan tried not to think about it.

On Sunday afternoon, Jamey begged Ryan to go to the park with him and help him practice baseball. His Little League games didn't start until spring, but with their dad away so much, it was a novelty to have an older boy to work with.

"Basketball's my game," Ryan told Jamey after he had pleaded for Ryan to come to the park.

"Aw, so what? I'll bet you could pitch really well if you try."

Ryan smiled at Jamey. "Can Jordan come, too?" he asked.

"She's no good. She couldn't hit a baseball if it were the size of a blimp."

Jordan glared at her brother, but she had to admit that Jamey was right. "It's okay," she said. "I'm really not much on a baseball diamond."

"Come on," Ryan urged. "Show me."

The three of them meandered down to the park. The sun shone, taking the November chill out of the afternoon. Jordan stepped up to home plate, gripping the bat for dear life. "I don't mind catching in the outfield," she told Ryan nervously. "Why don't you let Jamey bat first?"

"Naw. I'll pitch and Jamey can go to the outfield. I want to see your stuff."

Jordan knew that her "stuff" wasn't much. "Well, all right," she said. "But promise not to laugh."

"My snake can swing better than she can," Jamey yelled as he walked toward the outfield.

"Let's give her a chance," Ryan said, and Jamey did as he was told. "Take a few swings," Ryan instructed, heading for the pitcher's mound.

He lobbed a ball and Jordan swung wildly in the air. "See what I mean?" she said.

"Try again."

She did, but the ball hit the chain-link fence behind her as her bat took another swipe at the air.

From the outfield, Jamey shouted, "See what I mean? She's hopeless!"

"Cool it, muffin brain!" Jordan yelled.

"You've just never had proper coaching," Ryan told her, jogging up to the batter's box. He stood behind her, lifted the bat, and fitted her hands securely on the wooden handle. "Grip it this way. And don't chop at the ball when it comes over the plate. Swing in one smooth motion." He helped her swing the bat at the air a few times. Then he called, "Okay, Jamey. Toss us a few."

Jamey pitched, and with Ryan directing the bat, Jordan connected with the ball. The vibration from the wood stung her hands. The ball flew high and far, and Jamey scrambled after it. "That's the first decent ball I've ever hit!" Jordan beamed.

"All right. Now try it on your own. Remember what I told you."

She missed his first two pitches, but hit the third one hard down the third base line. Jamey chased it as Jordan flashed Ryan a pleased smile. He offered a thumbs-up signal, and she leaned back on the bat, feeling satisfied with herself.

She studied him and remembered the feel of his arms around her when he was showing her how to bat. His arms had felt big and warm. *Where are the bells and whistles?* Jordan asked herself. There weren't any. Jordan couldn't understand why. Ryan Elliot was good-looking, shy, but friendly, and very, very nice. But there was no quivery feeling in the pit of her stomach when she was with him.

Jordan knew that those crazy sensations didn't automatically mean a person was in love, but they did mean that the person you were with was special, different from all others. She thought about it for a minute. She should be head-over-heels crazy for Ryan. She should be doing everything in her power to make him like her as a girlfriend before school started back up. Why wasn't she?

"Let me go to the outfield and let Jamey bat," she called to Ryan. Jordan dropped the bat and headed for the outfield. Maybe she could figure out her feelings out there.

Jamey tossed her his glove as he galloped past. She reached the outfield and studied Ryan on the pitcher's mound. He was big, blond, and good-looking. *What's wrong with me?* she wondered.

Nine

"YOU look different," Laurie said in the hall on Monday.

"How so?" Jordan asked.

"I'm not sure . . ." Laurie looked carefully at her friend for a long moment. "Sort of healthy."

Her evaluation surprised Jordan. "I don't know why. I ate like a pig over the holidays. And I don't think the jogging would have an effect already."

"You've been jogging?" Laurie raised a skeptical eyebrow.

"Ryan's been jogging. I've just been tagging along."

"How romantic!" Laurie bubbled.

"There's nothing romantic about sweating."

Laurie craned her neck, glancing over students talking in the halls and waiting for the bell to ring. "Where is Ryan anyway? I can't wait to meet him. And I'll bet Jennifer's about to pop her buttons over seeing him."

At the mention of Jennifer, Jordan felt tense. Why was everyone so interested in her business anyway? "He's in the office with his mother getting his schedule taken care of."

"Maybe you'll get lucky and have the same lunch period like me and Wade. Then you can eat together."

"We already eat together at breakfast and dinner. I think I can make it through lunch without his company."

"But isn't it wonderful living under the same roof with your boyfriend? I mean, it seems so romantic to think that the first person you see every day is the person who means the most to you. What's it like, anyway?"

"It's like having to share an already over-crowded bathroom with another boy. And never having any privacy."

Laurie's eyes had grown wide. "Gee, I never dreamed it could be that way."

"Well, it can be."

"But—but he's your *boyfriend*," Laurie wailed. "It should be wonderful having him around all the time. You get to talk to him whenever you want. Wade and I talk on the phone so much that my mother sets the kitchen timer whenever he calls. We only can talk ten minutes or so," she complained.

Jordan decided she'd laid it on too thick. "Well, it is fun most of the time," Jordan admitted. She thought about how much fun Ryan could be when they went to the park or played a board game. "Forget I complained," she added. "But constant togetherness can get old. Just remember what I told you if you ever get tired of Wade."

"I've got an idea!" Laurie's voice sounded excited. "Why don't you and Ryan meet Wade and me at the Palace after school today? That way we can all get to know each other better."

A sinking sensation gripped Jordan's stomach. Jordan had hoped that she would be able to put off a trip to the Palace. She didn't want kids talking about her and Ryan. What if he heard about their "romance"? She licked her lips nervously. "Gee . . . I don't know . . ."

"Aw, come on. You can't keep him to yourself forever. And besides, you need to introduce him around. Wade wants to meet him, too."

Laurie made sense. If Jordan's primary goal was to make sure Ryan made friends, then it was up to her to make sure that people met him. "I guess we could walk over there after school," she said. "We'll have some ice cream and let Ryan meet the gang."

"Great! We'll see you there."

The warning bell rang and both girls headed off in different directions. The rest of the day was worse than she had imagined. The new boy in school—Jordan's boyfriend—was the talk of the eighth grade. Jordan saw kids whispering and pointing. Once, she passed Ryan in the corridor and heard a group of girls giggle.

"Hey," he said, "meet me after school and we'll walk to the bus stop together. I'm afraid I might get lost without a guide."

"Actually, I was going to take you to the Polar Palace," Jordan said. "It's a Martin hangout. Plus my friend Laurie wants to meet you."

"That's even better," Ryan said. "I'd like to meet some other kids. So far, it's weird going to classes and not knowing anyone. Your face is the first familiar one I've seen all morning."

"Then it's the Palace for a round of ice cream. See you later," Jordan said, hurrying off. Now there was nothing left to do but hope for the best.

◆ ◆ ◆ ◆

The Polar Palace was crowded when Jordan and Ryan entered. The smells of vanilla and hot fudge made her mouth water.

Laurie waved to them from a back booth, and the couple made their way through the crowd. Jordan's eyes darted nervously around, searching for Jennifer, but she didn't see her. She was so relieved that she sighed out loud. Jordan felt she could fake her way through a session with Laurie, but facing the third degree from Jennifer was another matter.

After introductions, she leaned over and asked, "So, where's Princess Jennifer? I thought for sure I'd stumble over her when I came through the door."

"She and Glen broke up. And you know Jennifer—she lays low until she has someone to impress us with."

"Maybe we won't see her for the rest of the year then," Jordan said dryly.

A waitress came to their table. "What'll it be?"

Jordan pointed to the menu printed on the placemats, and Ryan studied the offerings. "What's a Hog Wallow?"

Wade said, "A Texas-sized bowl of ice cream."

"It says it's only for big ice cream lovers. Do you all want to get one?"

Jordan opened her mouth to explain something, but Wade and Laurie flashed her a look. Wade said, "I'll split the cost of one with you. But you've got to finish the whole thing."

Ryan looked doubtful. "A bowl of ice cream? I won't have any trouble. I hope there's enough for the rest of you."

The other three exchanged glances. "We'll take small bites," Jordan told him, suppressing a smile.

After the waitress left, Wade turned to Ryan. "So how do you like living here so far?"

Ryan shrugged. "It's all right. And school's school."

"Yeah, but getting to live with Jordan and to see each other every day . . .," Laurie interjected.

Ryan gave her a questioning glance. "So?"

Jordan racked her brain for a way to steer the conversation in another direction. "Did I tell you Ryan's a basketball player? He's very athletic."

"Really?" Wade asked. "Are you any good?"

"I'm okay."

Jordan scoffed. "He's terrific."

"Of course you would think so," Laurie said. "You're prejudiced."

Ryan turned toward Jordan. "Why are you prejudiced?"

Jordan ignored his question. "Isn't Coach Couchman looking for new players?" she asked.

"Coach is always looking for new players.

You should try out," Wade urged. "You've only missed about four weeks of practice. The first game is in two weeks."

"I don't know," Ryan turned his broad shoulders. "My mom hasn't found an apartment or a job. When she does, it may not even be in this school district."

"But you could play until she does," Jordan said eagerly, while hoping the conversation remained focused on Ryan and not the two of them.

"I'll think about it."

"Jordan says you two have been jogging together," Laurie commented.

"When she can keep up," Ryan chucked Jordan's chin.

"Did you jog in the Rockies? Wasn't it hard to breathe so high up?" Laurie asked.

"The Rockies?" Ryan looked confused. Jordan dropped her spoon to the floor with a distracting clatter.

Fortunately, as she bent to retrieve it, the waitress brought out the ice-cream order. The bowl of ice cream was huge. Ryan's eyes went wide as the huge bowl, heaped with every flavor of ice cream on the menu, was set on their table. The ice cream was covered with sauces, whipped cream, and chocolate and sugar sprinkles. Ryan's jaw dropped.

Every head in the room turned to look at the mammoth bowl. The waitress set four bowls and a pile of napkins in front of Jordan and her friends. "Enjoy," she said.

Ryan shook his head as if to clear it. Laurie and Jordan giggled. Wade grinned. "Do you think you can handle it?" he asked.

"Don't you guys do anything *small* around here?"

"Never," Wade said, placing his hand over his heart. "You're in Texas now. We don't know the meaning of the word."

Ryan gave Jordan an amused looked of resignation. "You knew all along, didn't you?"

"You said you were hungry," Jordan said. Her expression was pure innocence.

"I ought to smear this all over your face, baby Jordan."

Laurie looked from Jordan to Ryan and back again with a confused expression.

Jordan knew she couldn't explain. "It's a joke between us," she offered vaguely.

"It seems I overestimated my appetite and your Texas bowls of ice cream," Ryan said with a grin. "You're all going to have to help me."

"All right!" Wade said, and pushed his bowl forward for Ryan to fill.

"Ryan's super, Jordan," Laurie whispered to

her friend. You're sure lucky to have him as your boyfriend!"

All Jordan did was smile weakly. If only she could tell the truth.

Ten

BY the end of the week, Jordan had begun to feel more comfortable with Ryan at school. They arrived together in the morning and went home with each other every afternoon. By now there was no changing anyone's mind about their relationship. Jordan simply resigned herself to letting other kids assume they were boyfriend and girlfriend. She hoped Ryan never learned the truth.

She was completing work on a portion of the newspaper one afternoon when Ryan stopped by Mrs. Rose's room. "I'll be finished in a minute," Jordan told him.

"Jordan, I don't believe Ryan and I have officially met." Jennifer's sugar-coated voice flowed in her ear.

"Uh—Ryan, this is Jennifer," Jordan said tensely.

Jennifer beamed him a 100-watt smile.

"Jordan's just gone on and on about you. Do you like it here at Martin?"

Ryan nodded. "It's okay." His eyes took on a mischievous twinkle. "So what's she been saying about me?"

"Not a thing," Jordan interrupted quickly.

"Come on, Jordan. Ryan's all you've talked about for ages now."

Jordan could have choked her. But instead, Jordan said, "You know how it is. Talking about you beats talking about this newspaper. Jennifer, could you go to the teachers' lounge and give this to Mrs. Rose?"

Jennifer flapped long eyelashes in Jordan's direction. "Me? You want me to take it? Why can't you?"

"Ryan and I need to get home."

"Yeah." Ryan rocked back on his heels. "My mom had an important job interview today. I want to find out how it went."

"But I wanted to talk about the Rockies with you. I'm doing a report on them for my social studies class and I was hoping I could interview you."

Jordan bounded to her feet and thrust the newspaper copy into Jennifer's hands. "Go, before Mrs. Rose comes looking for it."

Jennifer put on a pouting look. "Honestly, Jordan Starling. You treat me like a slave."

But she flounced out of the room.

Jordan sagged against a nearby desk. *Boy, that was close,* she thought to herself.

Ryan screwed up his face. "The Rockies? Are you sure your friends know I'm from outside Washington, D.C., and not from Washington the state? I've never been east of the Mississippi until I moved here."

Jordan dismissed his concern with a flip of her hand. "Don't pay any attention to Jennifer. Geography was never her best subject." She scooped up her books and managed a big, bright smile. "Let's go home, and I'll make you a milkshake in the blender."

"That sounds safe enough. I still haven't recovered from the Hog Wallow."

Jordan herded him down the hall, half afraid that Jennifer would pop out at any second to do an in-depth interview with Ryan about a vacation he never had. She didn't breathe easy again until they were safely seated on the bus and headed home.

Later, in her kitchen, she scooped ice cream into the blender and then filled it with milk. "A Starling original," she told Ryan while he watched. "Do you want a banana in it?"

"Sure." He paused for a minute. "You know I've been thinking . . ."

"Sounds dangerous."

"I think I will go out for the basketball team."

"That's great!" Jordan said. "I'll come and cheer for you. What if your mother moves before school's out?"

"I don't know." He shook his head and his blond hair shimmered. "All I know is that I'd like to play. But first, I'll have to make the team."

"No sweat. One of our reporters just did a news story that said that the team isn't doing very well. A couple of players quit." She turned on the blender, but the ring of the phone made her turn it off immediately. She picked up the receiver. A man's voice asked for Ryan. Jordan could tell by the crackle on the line that the call was long-distance. "For you," she said to Ryan.

Ryan took the phone carefully, as if it might bite him. She heard him say, "Hello. Oh . . . hi, Dad." Then there was silence. "Yeah, things are fine." There was another pause. "She's doing all right. No job yet." Jordan saw that Ryan's knuckles had turned white from holding the receiver too tightly. "Sure. I'll write. Bye." Ryan hung up, and the air in the room seemed to grow thick and heavy. Jordan swallowed hard. She wasn't sure what to do or say.

74

Suddenly Ryan bolted from the room. "I'm going jogging."

She scampered after him. But he'd darted up the stairs and into his room before she could catch him. In minutes he came out, dressed in sweats and a headband. His face looked pale and pinched.

"Wait a minute and I'll go with you," she offered.

"No," he said. "I want to go alone." He brushed past her on the landing.

"But your milkshake . . ."

"I don't want a stupid milkshake! Tell Mom I don't know when I'll be back," he called over his shoulder as the front door slammed behind him.

Shaken, Jordan returned to the kitchen. She glared at the phone. In one brief minute, Ryan's great mood had turned dark. She felt awful for him. And she hated Ryan's father for making it happen. She stared down into the blender, where the ice cream and banana floated in milk. Then she dumped the mess into the garbage disposal.

◆ ◆ ◆ ◆

"Are you still speaking to me?"

Ryan's question caused Jordan to glance up

from her intense study of the back of the cereal box the next morning at breakfast. He'd come in the night before and gone directly to the room he shared with Jamey and spent all evening there. Jordan had explained to Mrs. Elliot what had happened. "Ryan has to work it out for himself," she'd told Jordan. "I wish I could do it for him, but I can't."

"Of course, I'm still speaking to you," Jordan said. "Would I complain because you left me behind and went jogging alone?"

He dropped his gaze. "I didn't mean to be rude."

"No big deal. Here, have some cornflakes."

"Regular or Texas-sized?" Jordan laughed and pushed the box of cereal toward him. "Where is everybody?" he asked.

"Mom's taken Jamey to school because his class is going on a field trip and she's a driver." She licked her lips and chose her next words carefully. "Is everything all right now?"

Ryan's eyes turned cloudy. "I just wasn't expecting my dad to call. It caught me off guard."

"Don't you miss him?"

Ryan stared absently into space. "We did everything together. He took me to all my games and cheered in the stands for me. But I feel like he dumped me when he moved out."

"Even so, he *did* call you," Jordan pointed out. "I'll bet he misses going to your games, too."

"Big deal."

She cleared her throat and decided to change the course of the conversation. "Are you still going out for the basketball team?"

"Yeah. I am."

"Good. Maybe I'll do an interview with you for the school newspaper."

"As long as I'm on your good side," he said, "how about ten extra minutes in the bathroom in the morning?"

"Watch it, buster! Don't get pushy."

"Sorry. I lost my head."

Their eyes locked, and Jordan felt a warmth for him flood through her. He wasn't her boyfriend in the way that Wade was Laurie's. But Ryan Elliot was becoming more and more special to her. She had to admit that she cared about him in ways she'd never cared about anyone else. She only wanted the best for him. "Come on," she said, breaking the silence. "We'd better get to school before they think we're skipping classes."

He darted to the door. "Last one to the bus stop has to jog an extra ten laps around the park tonight."

She bounded after him into the sunlight.

Eleven

RYAN made the basketball team the same
day his mother landed a job with a pres-
tigious law firm. Jordan's mother celebrated
by ordering a cake from the bakery that announced "Congratulations to the Elliot Team!"
in mounds of sugary green icing. As they sat
at the dinner table and passed around slices
of the dessert, Ryan asked, "Should I start the
season if we might be moving soon?"

"Absolutely," his mother told him. "I don't
think we'll move right away. We'll stay here
until I can save up a few paychecks. Then I'll
look for an apartment and arrange to have
our furniture shipped from Virginia. You go
ahead and play basketball."

Jordan had mixed emotions. She liked
Ryan. She liked his mother. But it was becoming harder to keep pretending he was her
boyfriend to her friends at school. Still, if he

moved, she knew she'd miss him terribly. "I'll be in the bleachers to cheer for you, Ryan," Jordan said.

"Aw, that's okay. You don't have to waste your time after school going to my games. I know you're busy with the newspaper."

"Well, with your mom working, I figure she can't come to cheer. So I'll do it for her. Besides, I'd like to see you play."

"You wouldn't mind?"

"Not a bit. Martin hasn't had a winning season in years. Maybe you'll be our good-luck charm."

"Yeah," Jamey interrupted. "With Jordan yelling in the bleachers, it'll scare the other team off."

Jordan shot Jamey a murderous glance as he doubled over laughing at his own joke.

After cake and ice cream, Jordan put on her jogging clothes and ran with Ryan to the park. A numbing December chill set her teeth chattering. She tugged her knit cap lower over her ears and paused to rest on a bench near the play area. "Boy, it's cold. Just think, Christmas is only a few weeks away." Then she saw the sad look on Ryan's face. She cleared her throat. "Is everything all right?"

"Sure."

She watched him scuff the toe of his

running shoe in the hard-packed earth. "You don't act like everything's all right. Come on, you can tell your old buddy, Jordan . . ." She regretted mentioning Christmas. She realized that it would be hard for Ryan to be separated from his dad over the holidays.

"I've never started a basketball season without my dad," Ryan said. His voice sounded shaky.

"Maybe you could call him and tell him about your making the team."

"Forget it. When he left us, I decided I never wanted to see him again," Ryan said bitterly.

"But he's your father," Jordan said.

"So what? He ruined our lives. He changed everything when he left us. Why did he do that, Jordan? Why?"

"I don't know," Jordan said. "But you live here now. And you just made the basketball team. And your mom's got a neat job. And you're doing great in school. Maybe that's enough for now."

Ryan said nothing for a long time. When he did speak, his voice sounded as if it were coming from a long way off. "Maybe it is." Then there was another short silence until he said, "When we get home, do you think you could make one of your special milkshakes?"

His tone was lighter, more positive.

"Only if you promise not to run off like last time. It was one of my masterpieces, and I ended up dumping the whole thing."

"Scout's honor," he said solemnly.

"I should make *you* fix it for *me*," she said.

"Tell you what," he told her. "I'll race you to the corner. If I win, you fix it. If you win . . ." He left the remainder of the sentence for her to complete.

"But you're faster than I am," she insisted.

He stooped to retie his shoe. "I'll give you a head start." He pointed to the side of the playground. "Start from there and I'll still beat you."

"No contest," she announced. She took one step and nearly fell. Glancing down, she saw that he'd somehow tied her shoelaces together. "Hey," she yelped. "No fair!"

"I'll meet you back at the house," Ryan teased as he started jogging away. The last thing he called was, "And remember, don't skimp on the ice cream. I like extra scoops in mine."

Jordan was so glad to see Ryan smile again that she didn't mind the trick he'd pulled on her. "I'll beat you someday, Ryan Elliot!" she shouted after him.

And, from a distance Jordan heard the sound of his deep laughter.

◆ ◆ ◆ ◆

Looking back over the holiday season, Jordan thought Christmas had gone well for both families. Her dad's arrival and the way he befriended Ryan in his open, good-natured manner, helped cheer up the Elliots' first holiday alone. Ryan's dad did send a box of Christmas gifts, and Mrs. Elliot placed them under the gaily decorated tree in Jordan's living room. But Jordan noticed that although Ryan opened all of his dad's presents, he put every one away. He never wore any of the nice clothes his father had sent.

Since most of the basketball games were after school, Jordan made it a point to be in the stands to cheer for both Martin Junior High and Ryan. The team needed all the help they could get. "They're not too good, are they?" she asked Laurie and Wade one afternoon as the team was being trounced by the opponent.

"Ryan's playing well," Wade observed. "He's already put twelve points on the board for us."

"Our *only* twelve points," Laurie grumbled. "Honestly, watching these guys play is like watching a rerun of the Three Stooges."

Jordan giggled. But her good humor evaporated when Jennifer shouted greetings to them from the floor of the gym. "Oh, no . . . she's climbing up to sit with us," Jordan groused.

Jennifer scurried up the bleachers with a flourish. Then she scooted between Jordan and Laurie. "I just love basketball," she said, ignoring the fact that there was no room for her on their row. Jordan felt like a sardine wedged in a tin can.

"Since when?" Laurie asked skeptically.

"Since I discovered Scott Lewis was playing center."

Jordan searched the court for Scott. He was tall and downright skinny, with brown hair and brown eyes. He was very shy and sometimes stuttered if a girl so much as spoke to him. Jordan liked him, but he didn't seem like Jennifer's type. "He's passing to Ryan, who's shooting a lot," Jordan observed.

"Yes, Ryan is saving us on the court today," Jennifer said, never taking her green eyes off Ryan Elliot. "In fact, Ryan's downright incredible out there. Did you see the way he dribbled around that guy on the other team?"

"So how long have you been interested in Scott?"

"Who?" Jennifer asked with a frown.

Jordan gritted her teeth. "Scott Lewis. You

remember . . . the tall guy down there in the middle of the game."

Jennifer's gaze never left Ryan. "Oh, since school started after New Year's."

"Two weeks. How nice," Jordan muttered.

"How's it working out with Ryan living with your family?" Jennifer asked.

"Fine," Jordan said with a vague toss of her head. "But why all this talk about Ryan? We should be talking about Scott."

Jennifer raised an eyebrow and turned her almond-shaped eyes on Jordan. "You never want to discuss you and Ryan, Jordan. Why is that?"

Jordan squirmed. "What a question. Just because I don't go blabbing my personal life to everyone . . ." She deliberately left the sentence unfinished.

"Well, it's just kind of weird."

"What's weird?"

"The way you and Ryan act around each other."

Jordan's heartbeat grew faster. "Oh? And just how are we supposed to act?"

"For starters, I never see the two of you holding hands or walking arm in arm or passing notes. You know . . . stuff like that."

Jordan felt panicked. She couldn't be found out! Not like this. And definitely not by

Jennifer. "So maybe we don't like hanging all over each other in public. Maybe we're more private."

"Just making a comment," Jennifer said with a sugary-sweet smile. "You and Ryan seem more like buddies than steadies. That's all."

Jordan stood up. "Things aren't always the way they look," she said. "Now, if you don't mind, I need to go to the girls' room."

"Hurry back," Jennifer called. "I'll let you know if Ryan does anything spectacular."

Jordan picked her way past a surprised Laurie, and hurried as best she could down the crowded bleachers. A roar went up as Ryan sank a shot from the far outside. She ignored the shouting and dashed into the restroom where she leaned against the concrete wall.

Jennifer's comments had struck on the truth. No, she wasn't Ryan's girlfriend. Yes, there was nothing more between them than friendship. But how could she ever tell the truth and hold up her head in school again? Jordan knew she couldn't. She was too much of a coward. She had to allow her friends to continue thinking that she and Ryan were nuts about each other. When would this mess end?

"It's got to be over soon," she told herself.

Soon Ryan's mother would find an apartment and they would move. Then Jordan could resume a normal life and no one would ever have to know.

Twelve

"**I** think we should have a party to celebrate making it through the first half of the school year," Jordan announced to her newspaper staff after they had finished the January edition.

"Sounds good to me," Laurie said.

"What have you got in mind?" asked Ken, a reporter assigned to cover seventh-grade activities.

"I'm open to suggestions."

Then Carmen spoke up. "It just so happens that I'm in the middle of planning my birthday party for next Saturday. I'm sending out the invitations tomorrow. Maybe we could make it one big blowout."

"Oh, I was thinking of something for just our staff. We don't want to horn in on your birthday party."

"Why not?" Carmen asked. "My parents

have already reserved time at a ranch nearby. There'll be music and dancing, food and goodies, and even a hayride once the sun goes down."

"Just a small get-together?" Jordan asked with a teasing hint in her tone.

"Well, you know how I like a good party." Carmen shrugged sheepishly.

"Don't be a drag, Jordan," Jennifer interrupted, her green eyes gleaming over the idea of a party.

Jordan frowned at her. "But what's it have to do with us working together on the newspaper?"

"Well, we could do something special before all the other kids arrive," Carmen suggested helpfully.

Jordan thought about Carmen's suggestion. "Like what?"

"How about horseback-riding? You all can come early enough to go out on the trail and have a picnic. Then we can ride back in time to meet kids as they show up."

"I like the idea," Laurie said eagerly. "Can we bring our boyfriends?"

Jordan stiffened. "I was hoping we could just be together as a staff . . ."

"Why?" Jennifer asked, wrinkling her nose. "Good grief, we see each other almost every day. I'd rather take a romantic trail ride any-time."

"I agree with Jennifer," Laurie said.

Jordan knew she was out-voted.

Everybody but her wanted to bring some-one else along. But if she brought Ryan, she'd have to pretend that they were an item with-out letting on to Ryan. Could she do it one more time? "All right," she finally agreed. "But let's keep the numbers down. This is supposed to be a *staff* party. Not a free-for-all."

But in spite of what Jordan had said, the entire staff invited friends to come along, and Jordan invited Ryan. The whole crowd was standing outside the barn while ranch hands saddled up their mounts. The weather had turned unseasonably warm. The sun shone, but the air still held a bit of a chill. Jordan took off her denim jacket and tied the sleeves around her waist.

"Ryan, I *love* your boots and hat. Are they new?" The way Jennifer cooed the words made Jordan roll her eyes in disgust.

"Yeah, I got them just for today. If I'm going to be a Texan, I thought I'd better look the part." His blue eyes danced as he looked at Jennifer.

Jordan tugged on Ryan's arm. "Let's go

riding, partner." Ryan grinned at Jordan, and Jennifer frowned. *Why can't she stick with her date?* Jordan thought. Poor Scott. Why had Jennifer dragged him along in the first place if all she was going to do was flirt with other guys?

Jordan swung onto a pinto that had soft brown eyes. Ryan mounted a bay, and together they trotted toward a trail that led away from the ranch and into vast, open plains. The sky was a hazy blue and the horizon was broken occasionally by mesquite trees and cacti. Jordan plodded along on her horse behind Ryan, inhaling the fresh air.

"What do you think?" she asked Ryan, indicating the land around her.

"It's different," he said. "And so flat. I've never seen land so flat."

"I guess it *is* different from the Rockies," Jennifer mused.

"The Rockies?" Ryan asked.

Jordan nudged her horse alongside his. In a loud voice she said, "Not as different as Washington, D.C., huh, Ryan?"

"That's right. I don't think I'll ever get used to how few trees there are out west."

"Who needs trees?" Jennifer quipped. "Give me the wide open spaces any day."

Then Jordan asked Ryan softly, "Are you

homesick?" Her face showed concern.

A small smile turned up the corners of his mouth. "Not really. I'm getting used to this lifestyle. I sort of like living here. It's different, but fun."

Jordan purposely slowed her horse, widening the distance between the two of them and Jennifer and Scott. "How's your mother's apartment-hunting going?"

"I think she found a place," Ryan said, turning to look Jordan full in the face.

"Where?" Jordan asked, trying to sound casual.

"Across town."

"Not in our school district?"

"No." He shook his head and a thatch of blond hair fell across his brow.

"Too bad," Jordan said. Part of her was relieved, but the other part of her would miss him.

"Maybe not."

"How so?"

"Well, my mom's asked your mom if I could stay at your house until school's out for the year. That way I wouldn't have to change school's again and I could finish up the basketball season. Who knows"—his grin flashed boyish and dimpled and he tipped the brim of his hat upward—"I might even go out for the baseball team. I practice enough with Jamey.

"I'll bet I could impress the coach enough to let me give it a try."

"Won't you miss your mom?" Jordan asked.

"Oh, I'll go stay with her on the weekends. I'll live at your house during the weekdays while she's working."

"Gee—that'd be terrific," she said weakly.

"Yeah," he said, his grin widening. "Do you think you could stand having me around until school's out?"

"No problem," her voice said. But her palms began to sweat. School wasn't out for months! Could she keep her secret that much longer?

"Hey, slowpokes! You'd better catch up!"

Jennifer's voice grated on Jordan's eardrums, but she glanced toward the sound and realized that she and Ryan had fallen far behind. "We're coming!" Jordan shouted back.

"Yeah," Ryan added. "Hold your horses."

The rest of the group thought his pun was so funny that they broke into laughter. Ryan clicked his tongue and urged his horse forward where he fell in beside Jennifer. She turned her most brilliant smile on him. Jordan could only watch helplessly as Jennifer bombarded him with questions, giggling and flirting for the rest of the ride.

The group stopped at a rock formation where they decided to eat their picnic lunch. The newspaper staff party wasn't at all as Jordan had planned it. There were so many outsiders that she hardly felt it was special for her staff at all. But at least the food was good.

Jordan was chewing a mouthful of fried chicken when Laurie sauntered over and crouched down beside her. Laurie whispered, "Doesn't it bother you that Jennifer is flirting with Ryan?"

Jordan stopped mid-chew. "Uh . . . what do you mean?"

"Oh, come on! Jennifer's been flirting with him the whole ride. Scott looks like a puppy who's been left out in the rain."

Jordan sighed deeply. "I'm not letting her bug me," Jordan said with a casual flip of her hand. "Don't worry about it, Laurie. It's no big deal." But Jordan was relieved when the picnic was over and they rode back for the birthday party. At the ranch, they danced and shared an enormous birthday cake with the rest of Carmen's guests.

The stars were beginning to appear when two flatbed trucks rolled up, each heaped with mounds of fresh hay. Hoping to separate herself from Jennifer, Jordan scrambled aboard the first one, dragging Ryan behind her. But although the truck filled up quickly, Jennifer managed to climb onto the same one and settle uncomfortably close to Ryan. Jordan sighed. She hoped that her friends wouldn't expect Ryan to cuddle with her as Laurie was doing with Wade. Jordan hoped she could survive the evening without anyone becoming suspicious of the truth about her and Ryan's *real* relationship.

Jordan snuggled deep into the hay, inhaling its sweet, dry fragrance. Beside her, Ryan nibbled on one long straw. "What do horses see in this stuff?" he asked.

Jordan giggled. Jennifer leaned over, resting her hand on Ryan's shoulder. "Isn't it romantic under the stars?"

Jordan felt panic sweep through her. She certainly didn't need a conversation about romance! And she didn't need Jennifer flapping her lips and eyes at Ryan all evening.

Thinking quickly, she grabbed a handful of hay and thrust it down the front of Ryan's shirt.

"Hey!" He yelped, grabbing at the front of his shirt wildly.

"Hay, yourself!" she called back, tossing a wad of hay directly into his face.

"This is war!" he cried.

In moments everyone in the entire back of

the truck was hurling hay at each other. Jordan twisted as Ryan shoved the scratchy hay down her back. She shrieked and rolled, bumping into Jennifer, who'd attempted to stay out of the way. Jennifer fell forward into an unladylike heap. She came up sputtering, spitting out mouthfuls of hay.

By now the hay fight had extended to the second truck and clumps of the dried hay were flying between groups. Soon there was more hay on the ground than on the truck. When the commotion finally died down, Jordan was weak from laughing and struggling. She lay back in exhaustion.

She watched Ryan crawl over to Scott and several other members of the basketball team to talk. And although quiet descended slowly on the trucks, the romantic mood of the night had been broken. Jordan was relieved. In the moonlight, she saw a pouting, sulking expression on Jennifer's face. Tufts of hay stuck every which way from her unkempt hair. The front of her shirt was smudged with dirt. *Tough,* Jordan thought. It didn't matter that Jennifer was miffed. What mattered to Jordan was that she had gotten away with playing Ryan's girlfriend one more time. Now all she had to do was make it until the end of the school year and she'd be safe.

Thirteen

"BOY, that Jennifer makes me so mad! How dare she flirt like she did with Ryan at Carmen's party? Who does she think she is anyway?"

Laurie and Jordan had paused at Laurie's locker on their way to the bus stop. "Calm down," Jordan urged, watching her friend fumble with the combination lock.

"Calm down? How can you say that? How can you be so calm after the way Jennifer hung all over *your* boyfriend?"

Jordan looked away from Laurie. "That's just the way Jennifer is. No harm done."

Laurie shook her head in disbelief "I don't understand you, Jordan Starling. Even if it is the way Jennifer is, she has no right to try to steal your boyfriend right out from under your nose."

Jordan couldn't think of anything to say.

She just squirmed. "And besides," Laurie fumed. "Ryan Elliot isn't all that innocent in this matter either. I don't think much of the way he acted around Jennifer. And with you right there by his side! That took real nerve."

Why can't people stay out of my business? Jordan thought. "Look, I'm willing to forget the whole evening. It was just one of those things, so let's forget it," she said.

Laurie removed her books, slammed her locker, and started back down the hall. Jordan hurried to catch up with her. "You're being too nice, Jordan," Laurie said. "Both of them are dirty rats in my book."

"Both of them?" Laurie hit the outside door and Jordan chased behind her into the weak January sunlight. "What do you mean, 'both of them'?"

"What kind of game is Ryan playing with you, anyway? You take him in, you help him get acquainted with all your friends, you make sure that he's happy, and then *bam!*" Laurie smacked her fist into her palm, juggling her books in the movement. "He dumps you and chases after another girl. Some boyfriend!" Her tone turned sarcastic.

It's not Ryan's fault! Jordan thought to herself. *He has no idea he's supposed to be loyal to me!* Aloud she said, "I wish you wouldn't make a big deal out of it. Besides, Ryan's mother's found an apartment and it's in another school district."

"Is he moving?"

"Maybe," Jordan said.

Laurie slowed down her steps. "You're too, much, Jordan," Laurie said. "If Wade had treated me that way, I'd be furious!"

"I—I just don't feel that way. If he really cares about me, he'll come back. I don't have to act hurt and jealous."

"Boy, are you dumb!" Laurie snorted.

"I am not."

"Fact number one," Laurie said. "Girls flirt. Fact number two, boys love to be flirted with. Fact number three, if you don't fight for what's yours, you'll lose it."

"All right," Jordan conceded. "I agree with your first two points. But I think that if you really care about somebody, you won't smother him. I think it's okay to give a person lots of space."

"Well, Ryan certainly has space all right," Laurie said grimly. She stopped dead in her tracks and stared straight ahead.

Jordan followed her grim gaze. Ahead in the distance were Jennifer and Ryan. They were walking slowly, holding hands. Jordan swallowed hard. Now what should she say?

Laurie touched Jordan's shoulder and Jordan stared into her best friend's blue eyes. "They're creeps," Laurie said. "Well, I promise you, Jordan, they won't get away with it." Jordan's pulse was pounding, but she couldn't think of anything to say. Then Laurie continued. "I won't let them get away with it. Not for one minute. Ryan can't just dump you because Jennifer batted her eyes at him. We'll fix them, Jordan. I promise."

Fix them? How was Laurie going to fix them? Jordan's hands turned icy. Suddenly it was as if she were living in a house of cards and a giant hand had sent the cards tumbling down around her. And there was nothing she could do about it, absolutely nothing. She mumbled good-bye to Laurie and stumbled on to the bus stop. Somehow, in spite of the sun and heat, Jordan felt cold—cold and scared.

The remainder of the week was a nightmare. Everywhere she went at school, Jordan could tell kids were talking about her.

Jennifer was home with the flu, so she missed the week of gossip. Ryan wasn't so lucky. Most people shut him out because they were on Jordan's side. Kids turned from him in the halls. They spoke only if he spoke to them.

Jordan begged off jogging with Ryan each

evening, keeping to herself in her room. She told him that she had a term paper to write. But the truth was, she couldn't bear to face him. Her friends meant well. But they were hurting him and it was her fault! She was lounging in bed the next Saturday, trying to decide whether to get up and face a miserable day of side-stepping Ryan or to stay put and avoid him. Sunshine shone through her window. Her clock radio played softly in the background. It would have been a perfect day. If only . . . A soft knock sounded on her door.

"Jordan?" Ryan's voice came through the door. "Jordan, are you awake?"

"Uh—sure."

"Can I talk to you?"

"Just a minute. I'll be right out." Quickly she tugged on jeans and a shirt and brushed her hair. Then she took a deep breath and opened the door. She headed for the top step of the landing where he was waiting for her.

"What's up?" she asked Ryan, sitting on the step beside him.

Ryan ran his hand through his hair. "Uh—Jordan, . . . can I ask you something?"

"Sure." She wondered if Ryan could hear her heart pounding.

"Have I got bad breath or something?"

Jordan smiled. "Of course not. Why would

you think something like that?"

"It's just the way everyone's treating me at school. Like I've suddenly sprouted two heads. Or gotten some sort of contagious disease."

"You're just imagining it. Everybody likes you."

He shook his head. "No, I'm not. Especially Wade and Laurie. They hardly speak to me anymore. I've thought and thought about it, but I can't figure out why."

Ryan thrust his hands into the pockets of his jeans and heaved a sigh. Jordan clenched her own fists, wishing she could erase everything she'd done. "Oh, I'm sure it's nothing. Wade and Laurie live in their own world most of the time anyway. Just act natural."

"I don't know . . ." His voice trailed. "I was just starting to feel like I belonged and then this happens."

"You do belong here," she said with conviction. "Just keep being yourself. There's nothing wrong with you."

"Positive?" For a moment, he looked hopeful.

"Positive," Jordan said, smiling.

He attempted a smile. She almost cringed with guilt. "Maybe things will be better by Monday," he said. "We have a game and I'm in the starting lineup."

"I'll be there to cheer."

"Thanks." He got up to leave. "And Jordan," he added, "thanks for being my friend. It really helps."

He left the landing, and she went back to her room and threw herself across her bed. Now she'd told another lie. She'd lied to him about what was happening at school. "What can I do?" she mumbled into her pillow. "How can I help him?"

She knew the answer, of course. But it was so frightening to her that she couldn't bear to think about it. Jordan leaped off her bed and paced the floor. She paused in front of her dresser mirror and looked at her reflection with a long, questioning stare.

Tell him the truth, her reflection urged. *He deserves to know the truth.*

"I can't," she whispered back. "What would everyone think of me?"

Fourteen

"LAURIE, please stop being mean to Ryan. And please tell the other kids to stop, too." Jordan's words to her friend came in spurts.

Laurie looked at her friend from her cubbyhole in the library. "Sit down," Laurie directed, looking puzzled. "And tell me what you're talking about."

For a second, Jordan's courage left her. It had taken all morning to get up enough nerve to even approach Laurie. But the miserable expression on Ryan's face when she'd passed him in the hall before lunch had told her that nothing had changed for him. The kids were still ignoring him. Jordan knew that she *had* to tell someone.

Jordan plunked down with a heavy sigh. "It isn't fair to have everybody mad at him."

"Is it fair the way he's dumping you for

Jennifer?" Laurie asked.

"There's so much you don't understand . . ." Jordan's eyes filled with tears.

"Hey, it's all right. You'll have other boyfriends." Laurie closed her book and patted Jordan gently on the arm.

"I'm not crying about losing Ryan. Oh, Laurie. Things are such a mess. How did everything get so messed up?"

"You've lost me," Laurie said. "What's such a mess? What are you talking about?"

"Ryan's not my boyfriend. He never was."

"Is this true-confession time?" Laurie made a stab at humor, and Jordan managed a wan smile. "I mean, do I have to take notes for the school paper?"

"It would probably be easier," Jordan told her. "A front-page story certainly would set the record straight."

"Why don't you start at the very beginning and tell me the whole thing," Laurie urged.

"You'll hate me. You'll think I'm stupid and vain."

"I doubt it. I think math class is stupid and I think Jennifer is vain. Can you top those?"

Jordan took a deep breath, rested her chin in her palm, and started, "It all started last summer when I came home from vacation. The whole trip was nothing but a bore!"

Jordan continued with her story, slowly at first, and then with more confidence. She left nothing out. She told how she'd tried to make Jennifer jealous over an imaginary boyfriend, of stealing Ryan's photograph, of her panic when she discovered he was moving in with her, of all her missed opportunities to set the record straight. She even told Laurie that she thought Ryan was a good friend, and that she didn't feel romantic about him at all. "Maybe it's because we were babies together," she said, wrapping up her story. "I mean we practically used the same teething ring. He's more like a cousin to me. I like him, but not in the same way you like Wade."

For a long moment Laurie didn't speak. She just sat there wide-eyed. When she did speak, she shook her head first, as if to clear it. "This sounds like a soap opera."

"Well, it isn't. It's real life. *My* life."

"And Ryan doesn't know?"

"He doesn't even have a clue."

"Maybe you should give up journalism and take up acting."

"I'll keep that in mind." Jordan chewed on her bottom lip. "What am I going to do, Laurie?"

"Well, first off, you don't have to worry about me saying a word about this to anyone.

Not even to Wade," Laurie told her.

"Thank you. I really would like as few people as possible to know about this. At least for the time being."

"But I honestly don't know how to make everybody back off from ignoring Ryan. Maybe if I put out the word that you no longer care about him . . ."

"No," Jordan interrupted. "No more lies. If I say I don't care about him anymore, it'll just sound like I'm jealous. The truth is, he was never my boyfriend."

Laurie squared her shoulders and looked Jordan right in the eye. "Then there's only one way to set the record straight."

Jordan let out a shuddering breath. "I know. I have to tell Ryan."

"I don't see any way around it, Jordan," Laurie said.

"Me, either. And believe me, I've tried to get around it for months."

"Maybe he'll laugh it off. He must like you as a friend."

"Yeah. He thinks I'm a great friend," Jordan said sullenly. "That's the worst part. First his father. Now me."

"What?"

"Nothing. Just some personal stuff he's told me." Jordan stood up. "Well, thanks for understanding, Laurie."

"No problem," Laurie said with a quick, open smile. "That's what friends are for."

Jordan left the library drained, but knowing she'd done the right thing. At least it was a start.

Now Jordan had a new problem—how was she going to tell Ryan? She just couldn't look him in the eye and tell him. There had to be another way.

When she came home from school, she waited in her room until she heard him come in from basketball practice. She watched him through a crack in her door as he wearily climbed the stairs and went into his room. Her heart raced as she quickly crossed to her desk drawer, fumbled through stacks of papers and keepsakes, and took out her diary. Clutching it tightly, she marched next door and knocked.

When Ryan said, "Come in," she entered. The room was darkened, the shades still drawn against the slanting sunlight. Ryan lay on the bottom bunk, tossing a baseball upward to where it thumped methodically on the slats of the overhead bunk. Jamey was at Little League practice. Ryan glanced at her. "If you've come to cheer me up, don't waste your time. It was another lousy day."

"I'm sorry."

"Don't worry about it," he sighed. "Look, Jordan, I don't mean to dump on you. It's not your fault the kids don't like me."

She took a deep breath. "You're wrong. It is my fault."

He stopped tossing the baseball and gave her a surprised look. Then he sat up and swung his feet to the floor. "What do you mean?" Her heart was pounding so hard that she thought it might jump out of her chest. Her hands shook, but she tossed the diary at him. He caught it, asking, "What's this?"

"It's my diary. I want you to read it."

"Aw, come on, Jordan—don't you think I have enough to read without going through your diary?" Ryan flipped it back to her. "I don't read girls' diaries."

She tossed it onto the bed. "Read this one. It'll explain a lot of things for you." She backed toward the door. "When you're finished, you'll find me in the park." Tears brimmed in her eyes. She scarcely made it down the stairs and outside.

Jordan began to jog. Blindly, she ran up familiar streets and past neighborhood houses. She jogged until her lungs hurt and her muscles ached.

At the park, she ran out of steam. A men's

league was playing baseball in the ballpark.

Children climbed on the jungle gyms at the playground. Jordan sat on a bench and traced patterns in the dirt with the toe of her running shoe. And she waited.

The sun sank lower. The ball game ended. New groups of children replaced the ones who had been playing earlier. She told herself, "He isn't coming." What seemed like hours later, she caught sight of him in the distance. He was walking slowly. The closer he got, the more uneasy she felt. When he arrived, she couldn't meet his eyes. She was so ashamed.

"I put your diary in your room," he said. His voice was tight.

"I'm so sorry, Ryan," Jordan said.

"I'll just bet you are!" he said harshly.

"Ryan, . . . please believe me. I never meant for it to go so far. Even now, I don't know how it did. I—I didn't mean to make up so many lies. But after the first one, I had to come up with another. And then another. And then it just kept building and I couldn't stop it."

"You could have stopped it any time you wanted!" His face had gone red. "All you had to do was tell me the truth as soon as I got here. We'd have had a good laugh and the whole mess would have never happened."

"Be serious," she almost shouted. "I didn't

know you. Or anything about you. How could I have told you? Would you have laughed?" She paused and he said nothing. "I didn't think so at the time, either."

"Then why did you tell me now?"

"Because no matter how hard I tried, I couldn't stop the kids at school from taking my side . . . from trying to help me keep you as my boyfriend."

"I guess you just ran out of lies."

His accusation stung. "That's not fair. I'm telling you now. Isn't that enough?"

"No," Ryan shook his head. "You pretended to be my friend. You acted like you cared about me, then you dumped all over me." His face turned gray. "You're no better than my father."

She wanted to hurl herself at him and scream, "Stop it! I am your friend!" But she couldn't move. It was as if she were glued to the ground. "No, I'm not . . ." By now, tears were running down her cheeks.

Either he didn't see them or he didn't care. "Well, don't worry about me, Jordan Starling. I can get along perfectly fine without you and without your friends." He turned and started off.

"Ryan! Wait, Ryan, please . . . I'm sorry." But Ryan didn't look back. Jordan was left standing all alone in the dust.

Fifteen

FOR Jordan, the rest of the weekend was a nightmare. She stayed in her room, cried, washed her face, and cried some more. If she passed Ryan in the hallway, he ignored her. She forced herself to sit with her family at mealtimes, but the food stuck in her throat and she didn't eat much. By Sunday afternoon, she thought it would be impossible to feel any worse emotionally. But she was wrong.

"Beth has an announcement to make," Mrs. Starling said over a home-cooked dish of bubbling hot lasagna.

Jordan glanced up and looked at Ryan. He sat hunched sullenly over his plate. Then she looked at Mrs. Elliot, who flashed a bright, happy smile. "I've put a deposit on an apartment and sent for my furniture from Virginia," she announced.

Jamey gasped and let his fork clatter to the table. "You're moving?"

"As soon as possible," Mrs. Elliot confirmed. "Don't you think I've sponged off you all long enough?" Her tone was teasing.

Jamey's attention turned immediately to Ryan. "But you're staying until school's out, right? Just like you told me."

"No. I'm moving, too." Ryan didn't even look up when he said the words. A surprised hush fell over the table and Jordan felt a sinking sensation in the pit of her stomach.

Mrs. Elliot gasped with surprise and asked, "But I thought you wanted to finish out the school year at Martin. What changed your mind?"

Tears pooled in Jordan's eyes. She knew why he wanted to leave.

"But you can't move!" Jamey protested loudly. "You said you were staying—"

"Well, I've changed my mind," Ryan snapped. "I want to go with my mother." He scraped his chair backward abruptly. "In fact, I'm going upstairs to start packing right now. The sooner we move, the better."

"B—But . . .," Jamey wailed, scurrying after Ryan. "You promised! You said you'd stay. Don't go, Ryan. If you stay, I'll let you keep my snake."

Uncomfortable silence settled in the kitchen.

"What in the world got into him?" Mrs. Elliot asked.

"Jordan," Mrs. Starling asked, "do you know what's happening?"

Jordan stared ahead of her and just shook her head.

"I can't understand it," Mrs. Elliot began. "All he talked about was completing the basketball season. What changed his mind?"

Mrs. Starling shrugged. "Who knows? Look, my husband will be back in a few days. Maybe he can get Ryan to open up."

Panic squeezed Jordan's heart. More than anything she didn't want her parents knowing the awful truth about her and how she'd hurt Ryan. What would they think of her? How would they ever forgive her?

"I don't know . . .," Mrs. Elliot said with a shake of her head. "Ryan's not too receptive about anything right now. I think he's very confused and hurt."

"Maybe all Ryan needs is time," Jordan heard her mother say. "Maybe he simply couldn't face the idea of your leaving him behind."

Mrs. Elliot furrowed her brow. "I just don't understand it."

Unable to sit still any longer, Jordan left both mothers and retreated to her room. She lay across her bed and cried a fresh river of tears.

◆ ◆ ◆ ◆

Ryan didn't return to school and Jordan explained that he'd decided to move the next weekend and was helping his mother set up their new apartment—which was the truth. Jennifer grumbled, "Well, he could at least call and tell me good-bye."

Laurie said nothing. Jordan realized what a good friend Laurie was. She knew the truth, but she kept it to herself.

When Mr. Starling arrived home in the middle of the week, he tried to talk to Ryan, but the boy refused to say anything more than he wanted to leave when his mother did. Jamey moped and complained, but he had no luck changing Ryan's mind either.

On Saturday morning, amid the hustle and bustle of loading Mrs. Elliot's car, Jordan refused to leave her room. She listened to the sounds of lifting and moving drift through the house. She heard Ryan and her father making trips up and down the stairs with boxes and suitcases and hangers of clothing.

Jordan's stomach knotted when her mother finally rapped on her door.

"Come in," her voice said. *Go away!* her mind yelled.

Mrs. Starling eased into the room. "They're about to leave."

"So?"

"So I think you should stop hiding in your room and come down and say good-bye."

"I'm not hiding," Jordan said stubbornly. "I've got homework."

Mrs. Starling lowered herself onto the bed, and Jordan felt her mother's eyes on the back of her head. "Can we talk?" her mother asked.

Jordan's mouth went dry. Slowly she swiveled in her desk chair and looked at her mother. "What about?"

Mrs. Starling pursed her mouth in deep concentration. "You know, Jordan, I don't like to pry into my kids' lives. I believe in letting you and Jamey work out your own problems. But I would always want you to come to me if you came up against something you couldn't handle."

"I would, Mom."

"It doesn't take a degree in psychology to figure out that something's going on between you and Ryan."

Jordan licked her lips nervously. "I—I don't

know what you mean . . ."

"You know why he's decided to move with his mother and not complete the school year at Martin, don't you?"

Jordan knew she couldn't lie. But the truth was stuck in her throat. If she told her mother, she knew she'd start crying and never be able to stop. "I—I . . ."

Mrs. Starling held up her hand. "I didn't come in here to pump you. In the long run, it's probably best that Ryan go with his mother now, anyway. They need each other right now. I won't ask you a lot of prying questions, honey. But I do want to let you know I'm here for you if you ever want to talk about it."

A lump swelled in Jordan's throat. "Thanks."

Her mother sat for a few moments, then rose and headed to the door. "But remember, Beth is still my best friend and we intend to see a lot of each other. In fact, your father has rented a cabin on the lake for the week of spring break and Beth and Ryan will be joining us for the vacation."

"That's great," Jordan said without much enthusiasm.

"Jordan, I know I've made a big fuss over you and Ryan being playmates and babies together. Maybe too much of a fuss. The two of you were really adorable together. But I can tell by looking at you now that you're not a kid any more."

"Yeah. I'll probably need a new bathing suit for the lake," she said with a self-conscious tug on the bottom of her shirt. What was her mother getting at anyway?

Mrs. Starling reached for the doorknob, paused, and asked in cautious spurts, "This thing with you and Ryan . . . it has nothing to do with your liking him . . . I mean, as a boyfriend, does it?"

Jordan felt color creep up her neck. "No," she said. "I—I like him. But not in that way."

Her mother smiled. "Good. Boyfriends come and go, Jordan. But friends are forever."

"I'll remember that," Jordan said.

"Now come downstairs and say good-bye," Mrs. Starling urged. Jordan couldn't say no.

On the porch, Jordan hung back, tucked slightly behind her parents and Jamey. Everyone waved as Mrs. Elliot's car backed out of the driveway. Ryan sat stiffly in the front seat. Mrs. Elliot honked as the car disappeared around the corner. Ryan never looked back.

Mr. Starling slipped his arm around his wife's shoulders saying, "She's only going across town, honey. Besides, spring break will be here before you know it."

"I know," Mrs. Starling sniffed. "But I will miss her."

As Mrs. Starling turned to go inside, she stopped at the door to stare down at her prized stone jar of brilliant red geraniums. The jar had stood by the porch railing for as long as Jordan could remember, holding whatever flowers were blooming in season. The jar had been carefully turned toward the brick wall of the house so that the jagged crack that ran its length was hidden as much as possible. "What happened?" Mrs. Starling cried in dismay.

Jamey tried to hide behind Jordan. "I accidentally hit it with my bat when I missed a ball Ryan pitched to me."

"Oh, Jamey . . .," Mrs. Starling said. But Jordan barely heard her mother and her brother. She stood gazing at the ugly crack. It exactly matched the one running through her heart.

Sixteen

A blazing Texas sun beat down on Jordan's back. Jordan was stretched out on the wooden platform anchored far out in the blue-green water of the lake. She'd been lulled almost to sleep by the soft lapping of the water against the sides of the platform and the warmth of the sun. From the shoreline, she heard kids laughing and frolicking in the water. An occasional speedboat zipped past, towing a skier. The platform swayed gently as waves from the boat's wake slapped its sides.

Jordan sighed contentedly. She'd only been at the lake two days, but already her skin had turned a toasty brown. Her new two-piece swimsuit fit her perfectly. Lazily she flipped over on her stomach, giving her back full advantage of the sun's rays.

She heard the sound of a swimmer approaching. She turned her face aside, hoping to discourage anyone from climbing onto the platform with her. She wanted to be alone. That's why she swam out in the first place. And since swimming was the only way to get to the platform, it didn't attract a large crowd. She felt the wooden planks sway as someone climbed onto the platform. A spray of cool droplets showered her. Then she heard Ryan's voice say, "Hi, Jordan."

Immediately she stiffened, rolled over, and sat up. His hair, slick and wet from his swim, caught the sunlight. "Hi, yourself," she ventured.

Until now, they hadn't been alone. They'd both been busy with the tasks of unpacking and settling into the cabin for the spring holiday. Jamey had monopolized most of Ryan's time and Jordan was grateful. That meant there was less time for them to think about how she'd destroyed their friendship.

"Long swim," he said.

"Too bad you had to swim all this way, and then find out it was me out here."

"I knew it was you. I wanted to talk to you."

"Are you going to toss me overboard and drown me?" she asked meekly.

For the first time, he smiled, showing his dimples. "No. I just want to talk."

"All right," she told him, not sure what she would say. Jordan waited for him to speak.

"How have you been?"

"Fine," Jordan answered cautiously.

"Did you make the trip here to the lake in the car with Jamey's snake?"

Jordan made a face. "Of course! That snake goes where Jamey goes. Jamey rode the whole way balancing Stallone's cage on his lap. He was so sure that you couldn't wait to see his dumb snake again."

Ryan offered a soft smile. "Yeah. Jamey's a neat kid."

"I guess he's okay," Jordan remarked.

"How's school? How's the paper going?"

"Really well. Mrs. Rose is entering it in some statewide competition for junior-high newspapers. We may win an award. I'm thinking about taking more courses in journalism when I get to high school." She paused for a breath. "And how's your new school?"

"For school, it's okay. I've made some good friends. I—uh—met a few cute girls, too."

"I'm glad. I—I never meant for you to have to leave Martin on such short notice. Or to mess things up for you and Jennifer, either."

"I never really liked Jennifer," Ryan confessed. "She was pretty and it made me feel good to have her flirt with me. But she's sort of an airhead. No offense," he added quickly. "I know she's your friend."

Jordan grinned. "She was never my friend the way Laurie is." For a moment, there was silence.

Then Ryan cleared his throat. "I also want to apologize."

"For what?"

"For the way I acted when I moved out."

"I'm the one who's sorry," Jordan said.

"And you tried to tell me that, but I wouldn't listen. I acted like a jerk."

"No. I deserved it. I made such a mess of things."

He dipped his head and chucked her under the chin. "Once I started thinking about it, I understood how it could have happened."

She blinked. "You did?"

"We all tell little fibs about things that happen—or don't happen—to us. I've been known to exaggerate my basketball skills to impress people."

"I exaggerated all right. I made up this whole story about a summer romance with a guy I didn't know except through pictures in my baby album."

Ryan squinted against the glare of the sun off the water. "You're an honors student, Jordan. What do you think the odds are for having the guy you made up such a story about actually move into your house?"

"Pretty big odds," she admitted.

"That's right. Just think, if you would have bet money on it, you'd be a millionaire. It's sort of weird if you think about it."

"True. But once it happened, I should have told you."

His expression sobered. "I agree. But you didn't and we can't change that." Jordan hugged her knees to her chest. "But," Ryan added, "you were my friend and you helped me through some rough times."

"I did?"

"You jogged with me, talked to me, set me up with all your friends. But mostly, you listened."

"I couldn't stand to see you hurting," she admitted. "How's it going between you and your father?"

His features turned dark. "I'm spending a few weeks with him this summer. I've had some talks with Mom and I know their divorce wasn't my fault."

"Why would you think it was?" Jordan asked.

"I don't know. My head was all messed up. I didn't know what to think. Or feel. I was so mad at them. Why couldn't they work it out?

They're supposed to be *adults*."

Jordan shrugged. "Grown-ups are strange. We'll just have to remember not to act that way when we grow up."

Ryan nodded in agreement.

A speedboat passed by, rocking the platform. "So is everything all right now?" Jordan asked after the boat had passed by.

"Things are fine with me."

"Are we—can we still be friends?" Jordan asked hesitantly.

"I'm counting on it," Ryan said with a warm smile. "Besides there are at least six guys back on the beach waiting for me to introduce you around."

Her eyes narrowed skeptically. "What do you mean?"

"I mean there are guys back there who want to know who the gorgeous girl is."

"Me?" Jordan's mouth dropped open in disbelief *Gorgeous!* Jordan had never even considered herself pretty. Jennifer was pretty. She was just ordinary. "I don't believe you."

Ryan rose and crossed his heart. "Then come back to the beach with me and see for yourself. They're really impressed that I know you. And that we're friends." *Friends*. Jordan liked the sound of the word coming from him. They were friends. After all, she'd known

Ryan for almost fifteen years! That was longer than she'd known anybody outside of her family. "Of course, for a small fee I can be persuaded not to tell them that you dump bowls of spaghetti on boys' heads."

"You wouldn't dare."

He poised on the side of the platform. "Only if I get to shore first."

He dove into the water, and she dove in after. Ever since she'd been born, she'd been tagging after Ryan Elliot. Jordan swam with sure, deft strokes. "I have a few stories of my own, you know," she called out. "Imagine not sharing your rubber ducky with a sweet, helpless little girl."

"Helpless!" he yelped, sending a spray of water into her face. She ducked below the surface and slipped around him, emerging a few yards away.

"You're not so tough, Ryan Elliot."

He grinned. "It'll be our special secret. Okay? I don't want to ruin my image with the women."

"Our secret," she agreed, stroking for the shoreline. She beat him by ten yards.